Thomas Rokeby

**The Diary of Mr. Justice Rokeby**

Printed From a Ms. in the Possession of Sir Henry Peek, Bart

Thomas Rokeby

**The Diary of Mr. Justice Rokeby**
*Printed From a Ms. in the Possession of Sir Henry Peek, Bart*

ISBN/EAN: 9783337019198

Printed in Europe, USA, Canada, Australia, Japan

Cover: Foto ©Raphael Reischuk / pixelio.de

More available books at **www.hansebooks.com**

# THE DIARY

OF

# M<sup>R.</sup> JUSTICE ROKEBY.

PRINTED FROM A MS.

IN THE POSSESSION OF SIR HENRY PEEK, Bart.

*Privately Printed.*

# PREFACE.

THE MS. from which this book has been printed is the Diary of Mr. Justice Rokeby. It is bound in leather, and the date 1688 is stamped on the back, as are also the letters AA under the date. These letters are evident proof of the existence at one time of more MSS. of this eminent Judge. It contains ninety-four leaves, the numbering of which commences on the third leaf. The two metal clasps which once kept it closed have been broken off. On the front cover the date 1 Mar., 1688, and the signature, Thomas Rokeby, are written, as is also the entry as given p. 1.

Thomas Rokeby, the writer of this MS., was the second son of Thomas Rokeby, of Sandal, Yorkshire, and a memoir of him, containing his journal, &c., will be found printed in the publication of the Surtees Society for 1861, ably edited by Canon Raine. He was born in 1631 or 1632. On 20th June, 1646, he was admitted a pensioner at Catherine Hall, Cambridge. In January, 1649–50, he became a B.A. At Christmas, 1650, he was made a Fellow of his College. The following extract from the Book of Admissions of Gray's Inn, vol. II., p. 1,051, shows the date at which he entered that Society :—

Decimo septimo die Maii, 1650.

Sol. 3 . 6 . 8. Thomas Rokeby filius secundus Thomæ Rokeby de Burnby in Coñ York Armiḡ Admiss̃ est in societatem huius hospitij die et āno sup'dicĩ.

THO: BRICKENDEN.

After he was called to the bar he seems to have passed a considerable portion of each year in chambers at Gray's Inn. His country residence when term was over was at York. He married Ursula, daughter of James Danby, of Newbuilding, Thirsk. He was the principal adviser of the Nonconformists in the North of England and took a leading part in the movement in favour of the Prince of Orange.

The entries made on the cover, the first leaf, and the first twenty pages were made before he was raised to the Bench, which took place on the 8th of May, 1689,* when he was placed in the Common Pleas, whence he was removed, 25th October, 1695,† to the King's Bench, where he remained till his death on 26th November, 1699. He was buried at Sandal, near Doncaster.

Full particulars as to his family, &c., have already been printed in the publication of the Surtees Society which has been before referred to.

WILLIAM BOYD,

12, *Sloane Terrace, Sloane Street,*

*November, 16th,* 1887.                               *London, S.W.*

*Facsimile of Signature*

---

\* *Vide* Patent Roll, 1 William and Mary, Part 3 (24).

† *Vide* Patent Roll, 7 William III., Part 4 (26).

*On the front inside cover.*

## A A

1: Mar: 88:

6. Aug. 88. ret. ⅌ Wade & Dixon v' Hilton

*On the first fly-leaf.*

Ebor: Ass: 8: Mar: 8⅞:

Justices of Assize Just. Lutwich & Baron Tho. Powell

Ebor: Ass: 28. July: 88

Just⁸ of Assize Ld. Ch: J: Wright & Just: Jennor

*On the back of the first fly-leaf.*

Ebor: Ass: 8. Mar. 8⅞

City. tryed: 12:

County entred; 151

tryed 103

*(in pencil)* Ebor: Ass: 28. July: 88

City tryed: 10

County entred: 159

tryed: 120

B

**A. A.**

8 Mar: 8⅞.

Arnold & Johnson, p. q̃. 2.

Acklam & Cross, p. d. 1.†

28 July, 88.

Adams & Welfitt p. d. 1.

Atkinson & Hunter, p. q̃.

**B. B.**

Barber *v* Tomson, Constable et al. p. q̃: r: 1.

8 Mar. 87.

Birkby *v* Errick et al. p. d: ²2.

Idem & Exley, p. d. 1.

Birtby & Hicks, p. d. 1.

5 Apr. 88,  ret.‡ p. Bullock *v* Clerk: r.

24 July, 88,  Blakiston & Wolfe, p. q̃: r.

25 Jul:  Bell & Robinson p. q̃. r. 1.

Baines & Belwood, p. d. ½, 1, & ½.

Bentley & Hillary, p. q̃: r: r:

28 July, 88.

Bamforth & Eyre, p. q̃: 1.

Burman & Plant, p. q̃. 1.

Breares & Cloudesly, p. q̃: 1.

Bernard & Wilkinson, p. d. 1.

---

* p. q̃. 2·=pro querente. 2 [guineas].     † p. d. 1.=pro defendente.  1 [guinea].
‡ ret.=retained.

Barber & Hogg, p. q̃. 1.

Booshman & Dixon, p. q̃. 1.

Belwood & Donford, p. q̃. 1.

### C. C.
8 Mar 87.

Currer & Green, p. q̃. 2.

Carter & ux vᵉ Palliser et al. p. q̃. 1.

Carver & Savile, p. q̃. 2.

Close & Gilling, p. d. 1.

31 Mar 88     ret. p. Fran. Cooper vᵉ Rich. Blyth, *pr. terrs.* in West-Cottinwith.

28 July, 88.

Catlin & Peirson, p. q̃. 2.

Carter & Hunton, p. d.

2 Feb: 88:     Cambell & Atkinson, Ejec. p d. ret. p Mʳ Ridsdale.

4

### D. D.
8 Mar 87.

Danby & Gilling, p. d: 2 Mar: 87.

Dawes & Swinburn, p. d. 1.

Dowker & Micklethwait, p. q̃. 1.

28: July: 88.

Dawes & Swinburn, p d. 1.

Daniell & Thompson et al. p d. 2.

Dixon & Hitch, p q̃. 2.

### E. E.
28 July: 88.

Ellis & Peñyman, p. d. 1ˢ.

Elcook & Easby, p. q̃. 1.

6

## F. F.

Fairfax dñs* $v^a$ Emerson et al. p q̃. r. 1. 5 Mar. 8 Mar: 87.

Fost' & Bird et al. p. d. L. D. 1.

Frogmorton & Hodgson, p. d. 1.

Fox & Huby, p. q̃. 2.

1 Nov: 88   Feilding & Baldero, p. d.

## G. G.

Gordon & Peñyman, p. d. r. 6 Mar.

Gamble & Calvert, p. d. 1.

8

## H. H.

8: Mar: 87.

Halliday & Ingleby, p. q̃. 2.

Hesslerig et al. $v^a$ Episc: Durhã et al. p. q̃. 4.

Hebden & Overton, p. q̃. 2.

Hardwick & Yoward, p. d. 1.

Horsley & Wilkinson, p. Deft. 1.

Haugh & Moore, p. q̃. 1.

Hodgson & Maddison, p. q̃. 2.

Hirst & Duffeild, p. q̃. 2.

Heslerig et al. $v^a$ Episc: Durhã et al. p. q̃. '1 2'.

28 July, 88.

Hagg & Wild, p. q̃. 2.

Hall & Birkhead, p. q̃. '1.

Holdgate & Garton, p. q̃. 1.

Helper & Thompson p. q̃. 1.

Hesslegrave & Peirson, p. d. 1.

* Dominus.

Hobson & Winpeñy, p. d. 2.

Headly & Atkinson, p. q̃. $1.

Sept: 4: 88, ret. p heires att Law of M$^r$ Harrison of Cayton.

Harpar & Paul, p. d.

J. J.

9

8 Mar 87.

Iles & Laycock, p. d. 1.

28 July: 88.

Jackson & Bagwith, p. q̃. $1.

Jackson & Norfolk, p. d.

10

K. K.

Y$^e$ King $v^s$ Northrideing, p. d. r. 2: 2 Mar: 87.

Y$^e$ King $v^s$ Wiñard, p. d. r$^r$: 6 Mar.

Knight & Wilson, p. d. r. 1. 7 Mar.

8 Mar: 87.

28 July, 88.

Y$^e$ King & Peacock, p. q̃.

L. L.

11

8 Mar 87.

Lodge et al. $v^s$ Bayock, p. d. r$^r$: 6 Mar.

Lavender & Crooke, p. q̃. 1. 1.

17 May, 88, ret. p. Geo: Lofthouse $v^s$ Ric$^d$ Lofthouse.

24 July, 88, Lemair & Tomlinson, p. d. r$^r$ $1.

28 July, 88.

Lavander & Barrowes, p. d. 1.

Laler & Pick, p. d.

12 .

M. M.

8 Mar 8⅞.

Morram & Thompson, p. d. 1.

28 July: 88.

Mould & Wharton, p. q̃. 1.

Mare & Cudworth, p. d. 1.

Maud & Noble, p. q̃. 1.

Mountain & Robinson, p. d. 1.

Middleton & Watson, p. d. 1.

Marshall & Vavasour et al. p. q̃. 2.

6 Sept: 88,    ret. p. Mᵣ Jo: More of Austrop, *in omnibus*.

N. N.     13

8 Mar 8⅞.

Nisbett & Carter, p. q̃. 1.

24 July 88,    Nisbet & Carter, p. q̃: r:

28 July, 88.

Noble & Maud, p. d.

Nettleton & Haigh, p. q̃.

14    O. O.

28 July, 88.

Osberton & Wilkinson, p. q̃. 1.

Oates & Dun, p. d. 2.

P. P.     15

9 July, 88,    Polliser vˢ Hund. Bulmer, p. q̃. r.

19 July, 88,    Pinder & Andrew, p. q̃.

21 July, 88,    Precious & Jackson, ret. p. d. r.

28 July, 88.

Pape & Johnson, ꝑ. q̃. ret. L. D.

Phipps & Caley, ꝑ. d. 2.

16

## R. R.

8 Mar 8⅞.

Root & Guy, ꝑ. q̃—1: Scott.

Rawlinson & Tankred: 2: Ridsd$^{le}$

Robinson & Savile, ꝑ. q̃. 2.

28 July, 88

## S. S.         17

Snawdon & Gilling, ꝑ. d. r. 2 Mar 87.

Shuttleworth $v^e$ Scott et al̃. ꝑ. q̃. r. 5 Mar.

8 Mar 87.

Sinclar & Wiley, ꝑ. q̃. 2.

Swallow & Wheateley, ꝑ. q̃. 1.

Smith & Vesey, ꝑ. q̃. 2.

27 July     Shuttleworth & Scott, ꝑ. q̃. r.

Smith & Watter, ꝑ. d. ½.

28 July, 88.

Stafford & Hutchinson, ꝑ. d. 1. 1.

Shirt & Swift et al̃. ꝑ. d. 2.

Shaw & Williamson, ꝑ. d. 1.

Smith & Morland, ꝑ. q̃. $^s$1.

Stephenson & Chappelow, ꝑ. q̃. 2.

Spark & Empson, ꝑ. q̃.

Shuttleworth & Nicolls, ꝑ. q̃. $^s$1.

Seaton & Horncastle, ꝑ. q̃.

20 Sept. 88     ret. ꝑ M$^r$ T. Langley, ꝑ. Hen. Stapilton ads. Sand$^n$, s$^r$ demise. Jo: Stap.

18                 **T  T**

Thompson & Stubley, ꝑ. q̃. rʳ.

8 Mar 87.

Towars & Gilling, ꝑ. d. 2.

Throckmorton & Heaton, ꝑ. d. 2.

27 July, 88    ret. ꝑ. Tomlinson ads. Ingleby.

28 July, 88.

Thompson & Stapilton, ꝑ. d. 2.

Tucker & Clayton, ꝑ. d. 1.

Thruston & Kirton, ꝑ. d. 1.

Tranholme & Glover, ꝑ. d. 1.

Tomson & Stocks, ꝑ. q̃. 2.

23 Oct. 88    Thorpe & Empson, ret. ꝑ. q̃. r.


**U.  U.**             19

28 July, 88.

Vavasour & Hungate, ꝑ. d. 2ˣ 1, 1.


20                 **W.  W.**

Wright & Wyvill, ꝑ. q̃. instr 2. 7 Mar.

Wilkinson & Tyson, ꝑ. d. instr: 2. 7 Mar.

Wharton & Armitage, ꝑ. q̃. r.

8 Mar. 87.

Wharton & Crosby, ꝑ. q̃. 2.

Wood & Legard, ꝑ. d. 1.

Williamson & Lowthrop, ꝑ. q̃. 1.

Ward vˢ Baxter et al. ꝑ. q̃. 2.

Woolfgange & White, ꝑ. ᴅ. 1.

Wilkinson & Bernard, ꝑ. q 1.

Wells & Thompson, ꝑ. d. 2.

Wisker & Milson, p. q̃. 1.

Wrightson & Hardcastle, p. q̃. 1.

Apr. 5, 88      ret. p. Mᵣ Walkr vᵉ Hickson in Dowr.
28 July, 88.

Wallis & Robinson, p. d. r. 1.

Wrangham & Heslop, p. d. 1.

Woodhead & Bayley, p. q̃. 2ˣ.

Wilkinson & Bernard, p. d.

Waddington & Hey, p. d.

Wilson & Wyrley, p. q̃.

ret. p. Wade & Dixon vᵉ Hitch.

15 Apr. 89      p. Woods vᵉ Wainwright.

Sum̃er circuit, 93, Western circᵗ.      21

| | | |
|---|---|---|
| Winchestr causes entred | 26. | tryed—23 |
| Salisbury causes entred | 31: | tryed—26 |
| Dorchestr causes entred | 25 | tryed—22 |
| Lancestor causes entred | 55. | tryed—45 |
| Exoñ. Ch. Bar. entred | 12. | tryed—11 |
| Just. Rokeby entred | 8. | tryed— 7 |
| Devonshire entred | 90 : | tryed—65 |
| Som̃ersetsh : Wells, ent. | 69 : | tryed—51 |
| Bristoll, Ld. Ch : Bař : ent 18. | | tryed—18 |
| Tot : entred : | 334. | tryed: 268 |

In yᵉ whole circuit

| | | |
|---|---|---|
| Ld. Ch. Baron Entred | 171: | & tryed 139 |
| Just. R. Entred | 163: | & tryed 129 |
| | 334: | 268 |

*Page 22 blank.*

C

8: fine s$^r$ conč. Lond: Rich: Taylor & Ann his wife of 2 houses in Lond. for 500 y$^{rs}$.

Midš: fine Rich. Taylor Ann ux. & Ric. T. jun. to Wm. Tempest & Rob: Fowle.

Ebor: fine Jo: Fran: & Tho: Wildbore to Rob$^t$ Saintclare, Mano$^r$ of Knottingley &c.

10: fine from Hendrick & ux to Smith of Mess$^s$ in S$^t$ Andrews Holborn, Midđs.

3: Linc. Fine from Tho. Halcher et ux to Fran: Halcher of Lands &c. in Carby &c.

16: Fran: Stephens admitted guardian to Sarah Birch.

*Pages* 24, 25, 26, *blank.*

27

The 1$^{st}$ circuit after I was a Judge was sumer 1689: & I was to have gone y$^e$ Midland Circuit w$^{th}$ Baron Nevîle, but was Stayed in Towne to attend y$^e$ Parliam$^t$:

The times were thus:—

       Tuesday July 9, att Northampton.

       friday July 12, att Okeham.

       Monday July 15, att Lincolne.

       Thursday July 18, att Nottingham.

       Monday July 22, att Derby.

       Wednesday July 24, att Leicester.

       Saturday July 27, att Coventry.

           *eodem die* att Warwick.

The Judges hired a Coach betwixt them, y$^a$ costs of w$^{ch}$ & housekeeping, for my share thereof above all profits w$^{ch}$ came in throughout y$^e$ circuit was about 17 *li.*

*Page* 28 *blank.*

The 2ᵈ circuit Lent 16⅜⅜ Oxfordshire, I & Justice Eyre were to goe yᵗ circuit yᵉ times were

> Monday Mar: 3: Reading for Berkshire.
> Wednesday Mar: 5: Oxford.
> Saturday Mar: 8: Worcester.
> Wednesday Mar: 12: Stafford.
> Saturday Mar: 15: Salop.
> Friday Mar: 21: Hereford.
> Wednesday Mar: 26: Monmouth.
> Saturday Mar: 29: Glocester.

I went onely to Reading & Oxford, & then yᵉ King's pleasure was signifyed to me to returne to London, & Just: Eyre went yᵉ rest of yᵉ circuit alone, we had hired a Coach betwixt us, but Just: Eyre refusing to take it along wᵗʰ him, I came home in it, & after yᵉ circuit was over, yᵉ accᵗˢ were stated, & Just Eyre demanded that I should pay halfe of yᵉ charges of his own Saddle horse, & of his clerk of yᵉ chamber, & of his groome and Sumpter, I thought it was not reasonable, but upon his pposal, I referred it to Just: Powell & Just: Ventris who Judged it agᵗ me: & I was out of purse this circuit: 19 *li*: & above.

*Page* 30 *blank.*

### 3ᵈ Circuit, Suɱer. 1690.

The Lord Ch: Just: Holt & my selfe went yᵉ home circuit, it was appointed att 1ˢᵗ to begin in July about yᵉ usuall time afᵗʳ yᵉ terme, & soe were all yᵉ othʳ circuits, & accordingly were set up in yᵉ Hall Westmʳ & published in yᵉ Gazetts; but yᵉ French fleet comeing upon yᵉ

English coasts, yᵉ Queen by proclamation, 19 July 90, published an alteration of yᵉ Circuits by whᶜʰ yᵉ dayes for yᵉ home circuit were

Hertf. Monday 1st Sept. att Hertford.

Essex Wednesday 3 Sept. att Chelmsford.

Surry Monday 8 Sept. att Kingston upon Thames.

Sussex Thursday 11 Sept. att Horsham.

Kent Tuesday 16 Sept. att Maidston.

I hired two horses & a Coach this circuit & put my own horses to yᵉ wheele, & my charges in this circuit was above 25 *li*.

*Page 32 blank.*

ɩ

4ᵗʰ Circuit, Lent 169⁹⁄₀. 33

When yᵉ Judges chose their circuits in Hillary Terme there were 4 Judges chose their own Country circuits, viz. Lᵈ Ch J. Pollexfen, Ld Ch. Baron Atkins, Baron Lechmere & Just Ventris this made a great noise, & yᵉ Comʳ of the Great Seale tooke this occasion to find fault wᵗʰ yᵉ Judges choice, desiring by it (as yᵉ Judges suspected) that they might have yᵉ alteration of yᵉ circuits att their pleasure, & this was supposed to be done principally by yᵉ Ld Comʳ Trevor who was now made a Privy Councellor.

Yᵉ Queen had signed yᵉ fiat for yᵉ Judges comissions according to their own first choice, but by reason of sʳ Jo: Trevors complaint yᵗ he ought not to seale comissions to them to goe their own country circuits, yᵉ Judges (by yᵉ Queen's directions) altered their choice among themselves, wᶜʰ alteration was carryed to yᵉ Queen by my Lᵈ Cʰ. Just: Holt, & afᵗʳ she had approved it, it was sent by her to him agⁿ, & not to yᵉ Lds Comʳ of yᵉ great Seale, nor they did not meddle in making any alteration, but yᵉ Ch: J: sent yᵉ fiat to the clerk of yᵉ Crown, to make out, yᵉ Comissions.

34                    Lent 1690: 4ᵗʰ circuit.

This time my Lᵈ Ch: Just: Holt & my selfe went yᵉ Norfolk circuit, yᵉ days for wᶜʰ were

> Bucks, Thursday 12 Mar. att Aylesbury.
> Bedford, Saturday 14 Mar. Bedford.
> Hunt: Wednesday 18 Mar. Huntington.
> Canteb. Thursday 19 Mar. Cambridge.
> Norfolk, Monday 23 Mar. Thetford.
> Suffolk, Thursday 26 Mar. Bury Sᵗ Edmonds.

I hired a coach & 4 horses to my selfe this circuit, & took my chambʳ clerk (York Horner) in yᵉ coach wᵗʰ me, & hired a horse for Jo: to carry a portmantle, & I was out of purse this circuit in yᵉ whole about 34 *li.*                                             35

The matters hapening in this 4ᵗʰ circuit were not minded in due time to be set down.

36                    5ᵗʰ circuit Sumer 1691.

Just: Gregory & I went yᵉ Western circuit. The times were

> Southāptᵉ Wednesday July 22, att Winchestr
> Wilts, Saturday 25 July, att New Sarum
> Dorset, Thursday 30 July, att Dorchester
> Cornwall, Wednesday Aug. 5, att Launceston
> City of Exon, Monday Aug. 10, att Guildhall, Exon
> Devonshire, *eodem die*, att yᵉ Castle of Exon
> Somerset, Tuesday Aug. 18, att Wells
> City of Bristoll, Saturday Aug. 22, att Guildhal

I hired, a Coach & four horses to my selfe this circuit, & tooke my chamber clerk in yᵉ coach wᵗʰ me, & hired a horse to carry my portmantle, & I was out of purse this circuit in yᵉ whole about 13 *li.*

                    Sarum.                               37

Ejectmᵗ inᵗʳ Oakeapple & Beach for yᵉ Rectory of Orchestō Sᵗ George upon yᵉ demise of Tho. Curganven, clerk.

yᵉ lessors title was by reason of yᵉ deprivation of yᵉ defᵗ by act of Parlᵗ: for omitting to take yᵉ oaths to yᵉ K. & Q.

The defᵗ insisted that yᵉ lessor's Induction was not good, bec. yᵉ Archdeacon's Mandate to doe it, was directed *omnibus clericis et literatis infra archidiaconatū*, &c., & yᵉ clerk who gave yᵉ induction was not of his archdeaconry, & I doubting whether the authority was well executed in this respect, reserved this matter as a point to considr att London, but yᵉ plt. had a verdict for all, subject to a rule of Coᵗ to consider of that point.

*v.* Chris. Dean's case Noy. 134* & from him Dʳ Godolf: 280,† repert. Canonicū. yᵗ yᵉ Authority was well executed: & it was soe adjudged in Collys & Lant's ca: Hill: 6° Jac. rot. 190, B. R. upon a spec. verd. & according to yᵗ judgmᵗ I gave my opin. in this case.

*Page* 38 *blank.* /

29 July, 91. Sarū. 39 & 40

39 entred. 33 tryed by me.

Newman & Pinkney ejectmᵗ yᵉ plt: made title by a lease for 1000 yᵐ from Roger Pinkney yᵉ grandfathr to Rogʳ. Pinkny a youngʳ son of his, & Wᵐ Pinkny yᵉ lessor is admʳ of Rogʳ yᵉ lessee, yᵉ lease was dated in March 43: 3 witnesses, none proved him dead or their hands, possession for 40 yᵐ gone according to yᵉ lease.

yᵉ proof agᵗ yᵉ lease was one witness who swore that aftʳ yᵉ death of Rogʳ yᵉ lessee he was called to be an appraiser of his goods, & there was a scrivenᵗ one Brown who was imployed to looke into yᵉ writings & aftʳ search he told Rogʳ Pinkney he had roe title, & Roger asked him if he could not make one And yᵉ scrivener sᵈ yes he could make him

---

* Reports and cases taken in the time of Queen Elizabeth, King James, and King Charles, collected and reported by that learned Lawyer, William Noy (Attorney-General). London, A.D. 1656. 4°. 709. h. 3. British Museum.

† Repertorium Canonicum, &c. By John Godolphin, LL.D. London, A.D. 1687. 8°. 517. g. 29. British Museum.

a lease for 1000 y$^{rs}$ but y$^e$ witness said he expressed his dislike of soe wicked a thing & he knows not that any thing was done furth$^r$ by Brown but y$^e$ witness swore that att a form$^r$ Assizes he came w$^{th}$ W$^m$ Pinkny to y$^e$ chamber of one Wicks an attorny att Saru, who then read y$^e$ 1000 y$^{rs}$ lease to y$^e$ witness

anoth$^r$ witness proved y$^t$ Wm. Pinkny came to him & showed him a deed to w$^{ch}$ his name was put as a witn: & inquird of him if y$^t$ was his hand, & he could not say it was

3$^{ly}$ deft objected that Wm. Pinkny in y$^e$. 1$^{st}$ inventary of Rog$^{rs}$ estate in y$^e$ eccles. Co$^{rt}$ omitted this lease & aft$^{r}$wds put it in.

Jury foūd for deft. ag$^t$ y$^e$ lease & y$^e$ 40 y$^{rs}$ posess.

It was a slend$^r$ evidence y$^t$ y$^e$ lease was forgd Its fitt for a new tryall.

Jones & Gilmore ca: 41

For y$^e$ pew, verd p̄ q̃. ag$^t$ y$^e$ Evid. y$^e$ deft proved y$^e$ 1$^{st}$ erection of it by Phil. E. of Pembr: for y$^e$ dowag$^r$ of W$^m$ his eld$^r$ bro: who was deeply melancholy, it was before that 2 pews for y$^e$ wife's of y$^e$ copyhold ten$^{ts}$

this is very fitt to havė a new triall but y$^e$ K's Bench denyed it, bec y$^e$ dam̄s were but 2$^d$.

Rumsey & Herne in Trov$^r$ for Wood & Timber, a spec. verd. upon y$^e$ words of a will, whether they give a fee or an estate for life onely, I was of opin. it was onely for life: if it be onely an estate for life, judgm$^t$ must be p̄. q̃.

42          Wells 18 Aug: 91.

Biggs ag$^t$ Stibbs et al.

debt upon a bond ag$^t$ 5 administrators, 3 did not appear, 2 pleaded fully adm̄inistred.

y$^e$ plt: charged y$^e$ defts by an inventary exhibited in y$^e$ eccles. Co$^{rt}$ by y$^e$ procter of y$^e$ administrators, & a proofe made of y$^e$ com̄ission of y$^e$ administration to all y$^e$ 5 jointly.

yᵉ defᵗˢ offered to prove yᵗ yᵉ 3 psons who have not pleaded had got all yᵉ intestates estate into their hands, & yᵗ none of it came to yᵉ 2 now defts, and therefore they ought not to be charged, but I was of opin: yᵗ they all taking administration jointly, & exhibiting yᵉ inventary, they are all chargeable to creditors, tho 3 of them onely run away wᵗʰ yᵉ estate.

## Crofts & Dixon, C.B.      43

A specᵗ verdict att Wells, wherein all yᵉ circumstances of a quakers marȓ was found, & yᵉ q: was whethr this was a good marȓ. to intitle yᵉ husb: to be tenᵗ by yᵉ Curtesy, & I was clear of opin: yᵗ it was a good marȓ.

yᵉ naturall foundatiō of marȓ: is yᵗ pcreative appitite wᶜʰ is implanted in us by God, yᵉ desire of sexes, wᶜʰ is yᵉ effect of yᵗ comand & blessing, Increase & multiply.

yᵉ regulation of yᵗ appetite, & putting it undʳ morall rules, was by G's creating one man & one womā, to be mutuall meet helps.

  yᵉ solemne mutuall appropriation of yᵉ one to yᵉ other by their mutuall consents exclusive of all othᵐ, & consumating yᵗ consent by acts pp. for yᵗ relatiō make marriage

yᵉ essence of wᶜʰ is yᵉ mutuall consent to take each othʳ in yᵗ relation, & ye pformance of conjugall dutys.

yᵉ Cañons of yᵉ Ch: are but extrinsecall to it.

## 44

Mʳ Clerk yᵉ Lawyer in Somersetshire.

yᵉ Lᵈ Lieuᵗ powers were executed by comission to yᵉ Marq. Carmarthen, Earle of Devonshire, Earle of Dorset, & then all yᵉ deputy Leiuᵗ were put in in Councell, & they acted vigorously agᵗ yᵉ French in Sumer 90.

Now since y° D. of Or:* is Lieu'., he hath by misformat. (being a stranger) put in oth' men.

Sir Ed. Pheli: y° monster-children.

45

Att y° Nisi Prius in Midds 30 Nov: 91, before Just. Powell & my selfe.

Boddington & oth", adm" of — Boone, were ptts. ag' Tho. Sadler in an ač. of debt upon a bond of 500 ℔. entred into by y° de⁴ & 4 oth" to y° intestate.

Upon ñ č factū† pleaded

a speč. verd. was found y' y° def' and 4 oth" sealed y° bond in wh° they were jointly and severally bound to y° intestate y' before y° plea pleaded a mouse eat off ye seales of two of y° obligors, but y° oth' 3 (of w° y° def" [sic] is one) doe still remain on, & y° quest. was whether it was his deed or not:

I inclined to thinke it is still his deed, for it still remains y° joint & severall obligation of 3, & y° def' might have been charged w° y° whole, when there were 5 obligors, & may still be soe. v. 5, Co., 22, 119, Dy' 59,‡ 2 Bulst, 247.§ March: 95.

*Page 46 blank.*

47

Sixth circuit, Lent 169½. Home circuit.

Just: Dolben & Just: Rokeby. Y° times were

Hartford, Thursday Mar. 3, att Hatford.

Essex, Monday Mar. 7, att Chelmsford.

Surrey, Thursday Mar. 10, att Southwarke.

Kent, Monday Mar. 14, att Maidston.

Sussex, Friday Mar. 18, att Horsham.

---

* James, second Duke of Ormond.      † Non est factum.

‡ Les Reports des divers select Matters, &c., King Henry VIII. By Sir James Dyer, Lord Chief Justice, &c. London, A.D. 1688. Folio. 19. e. 10. British Museum.

§ The Reports of E. B. in the time of the late reign of K. James, &c. 3 parts. By Edward Bulstrode. London, 1657. Folio. 510. k. British Museum.

I hired a coach & four horses to myselfe this circuit, & tooke my chamber clerk in y° coach w^{th} me, & y° casuall pfits to y° Judges bore y° charges of o^r housekeeping & jorneys, except my coach-hire, w^{ch} cost me to Mr. Earle 13 *li*. 10*s*., & my Groom's horse-hire & charges about 2 *li*. 10*s*.

48

Att Hertford Just. Dolben entred 7 causes & tryed them all.

George Hadley, Esq^{re}, Sheriff. I tryed M^r. Benj. Cranmer upon two indictm^{ts}—1st, for drinking y° late K. Ja:'s health ; y° 2^d for words, y^t they can never make K: Wm. lawfull heire of y° crown. They turned K. Ja: shamefully out, & he swore by God he was for K. Ja., he being convicted upon both, I fined him 20. nobles upon y° first, & 20 markes upon y° 2^d, he being very poor; & I bound him to his good behaviour.

I condemned one Robber on y° highway for 2 severall robberys on foot.

49

Att Chelmsford I entred 31 causes, & tryed 24, but y° Sheriff had returnd 73 venires. Edw: Ford, Esq., Sheriff.

Wharton & Lisle, Trov^r for flax. Spec. verd. Y° Plt. is impropriator, & y° deft vicar of Thorpe. Y° q. was wheth^r Flax-tyth were small tythes or not, being sown upon 26 acres of land formerly arrable, y° whole parish being 1500 acres.

Oliv^r & Carcass eject: to try y° title of S^r Charles Terrill, Governor of y° free school in' Chelmsford. There was a gen. rule between Oliv^r & Blewet (y° casuall ejector) y^t Carcass should be made def^t & should confess lease *entre & ouster* generally. Then there was a spec. rule y^t y° def^t should not be pjudiced by y^t confessio to admitt y° governor's title ; but this being intituled a rule between Oliv^r & Blewet, y° plt. would not admitt it as made between y° now ptys. Y° deft offered to confess it if y° plt. would name y° governor, w^{ch} he refused to doe, & soe y° deft refused to confess, & y° pl. was nsuit for that cause.

50

Surrey.  Just: Dolben entred 20 causes & tryed 20.

Geo. Atwood, Esq., Sheriff.

M$^r$. Abell, undersheriff.  I condemned two men for burglarys, but att y$^e$ intercession of y$^e$ jury of life & death, I reprieved one for transportation.

51

Kent.  Att Maidston I entred 42 causes & tryed 35.

S$^r$ Jo. Marsham, Sheriff.

M$^r$. Pye, undersheriff.  Wintringham & Marsh, ejectm$^t$.  Y$^e$ q: was upon y$^e$ will ·of y$^e$ Lady Cater, whether she was *compos mentis* or not. Y$^e$ witnesses to y$^e$ will were y$^e$ Lady Man, M$^{rs}$ Kitchell, & y$^e$ D$^r$. Jacob, but y$^e$ Lady Man did not appear.  Verd. p. q̃. for y$^e$ will.  Y$^e$ onely land in q. was y$^e$ Mano$^r$ of Grove.  Y$^e$ p̃tt: made title to noe oth$^r$ lands by y$^e$ fine w$^{ch}$ he p̃duced.

Y$^e$ lands were M$^r$. James's lands who had 3 daugh$^{trs}$ of w$^{ch}$ y$^e$ Lady Cater was one, & one of them dyed w$^{th}$out issue.

52                              Horsham.

Just. Dolben entred 15 causes and tryed 13.

John Newnham, Esq., Sheriff.

M$^r$. Shepard, undersheriff.

.                                    *Page 53 blank.*

54

My Seventh circuit, Oxford Circuit, Sumer: 1692.  Just: Rokeby & Just. Eyre.

The times were thus

Berks, Tuesday 28 June, att Abingdon.

Oxoñ, Thursday 30 June, att Oxon.

Worcestr, Saturday 2 July, att Worcester.

City of Worcestr yᵉ same day.

Stafford, Wednesday 5 July, att Stafford.

Salop, Saturday 9 July, att Shrewsbury.

Hereford, Thursday 14 July, att Hereford.

Monmouth, Monday 18 July, att Monmouth.

Glocester, Wednesday July 2C, att Glocester.

City of Glocester yᵉ same day.

I hired a coach & 4 horses to my selfe this circuit, & took my chamber clerk in yᵉ coach wᵗʰ me, & my coach-hire, & yᵉ steward's accᵗˢ cost me above 32 *li*. over & besides all yᵉ circuit pfits, & yᵉ hire & charges of a portmantle horse in yᵉ circuit cost me above 4 *li*. more.


55

I began my jorney into this circuit from London on Monday 27 Ju. 92, & bated at Maidenhead, but yᵉ waters were soe great upon yᵉ road that att Colebrook they came just into yᵉ body of yᵉ Coach, and we were forced to boat twice att Maidenhead, & we boated yᵉ coach, & att yᵉ 2ᵈ time we boated o'selves, but yᵉ coach came through yᵉ water, & it came very deep into yᵉ body of it, & that night we lay att Henley upon Thames, where we were forced to boat yᵗ coach again, & att Henley there came to us two psons from yᵉ Corporatiō of Abingdon, who tooke care to pay all oʳ charges there, both for man & Horse.

Edw. Sherwood, Esqʳᵉ., Sheriff.

Mʳ. Greenway, a K's Bench attorney, undersheriff.

Here my bro: Eyre entred 16 causes & tryed 15.

We lodged at Mʳ. Green's house att Abingdon an old parliamᵗ soldier, a qʳᵗᵉmʳ, & now a dissenter called a Baptist.

56

Oxford I entred 10 causes & tryed 10.

Thos. Rowney, Jun., Esq., Sheriff, y⁰ son of an attorney living. Mʳ⸺ undersheriff.

We went from Oxford Friday 1ˢᵗ July in y⁰ afternoon & lodged att Stow on y⁰ Would in Glocestershire, where there is noe water but what they fetch halfe a mile out of town.

Saturday, 2ᵈ July, we bated att Parshoar, a place of y⁰ most beggars & y⁰ most confident that ever I saw.

Worcester.                                    57

Some pleased wᵗʰ my charge pticularly Mʳ. Walsh, a Just. of P.

Allen Cliff, Esq., a good Sheriff. Mʳ. Ashley, undersheriff.

Mʳ. Boweter, y⁰ Sheriff's chaplain preached an honest hearty sermon Lord's day afternoon.

Good Justs., Mʳ. Walsh, Mʳ. Bromley his son in law, Mʳ. Lechmere.

We lodged att an ancient attorny's house, Mʳ. Collings, nere y⁰ Coʳt.

Dʳ. Talbot, y⁰ D., a firme man to y⁰ Governmᵗ.

My bro. Eyre entred 21 causes, & tryed 15.

6 July we went from Worcestr to Wolverhamptō, 21 miles & bated, & yᵗ night to Stafford.

58

Stafford: I entred 38 causes & tryed 29. Gravenor Dyson, Esq., Sheriff, a mā firm to y⁰ Governmᵗ, but of small estate, soe we desired him not to invite us (as was usuall), & y⁰ next day afternoon dismiss'd him from attendance on us.

His bro: was undersheriff.

We lodged att one Barker's, a draper, a poor mā, & very strait lodgeing.

I tryed 2 or 3 causes of Saturday morning & went out of Town about noon, & came to Shrewsbury betwixt 6 & 7 att night.

59

Shrewsbury. Brother Eyre entred 71 causes, tryed 63. Thos. Wingfield, Esq., Sheriff, a Tory, as are a great pt of yᵉ Gentry.

Mʳ. — Tongue, undersheriff.

We lodged at Mʳ. Woolrich's, an apothecary. Good lodgeings.

Mʳ. Rowl. Hunt & Mʳ. Corbet, two good Justs. of P., recomended Robt. Clive, Jun., of Stych, to be a Just. of P. to act wᵗʰ Sʳ Jo. Corbett in a hand: where there is great want of Justs.

Sʳ Jo. Corbet, a firme mā to yᵉ Governmᵗ, not exact in his moralls.

Edw: Farmer of Bridgenorth, a parson deprived for refuseing yᵉ oaths, tryed for praying in his own house for yᵉ restoration of yᵉ late K. Jas. Found not guilty. Refused yᵉ oathes & I fined him 20s. for that.

60

From Shrewsbury we set out upon Wednesday noone, & came to Ludlow that night, 20 miles, & on Thursday we came through Leominster to Hereford, 14 miles, & were there by 12 of yᵉ clock. Dinmore Hill bad way. Att Hereford we lodged att Mʳ. Williams yᵉ Cler: of yᵉ Peace. Good Lodgeings. Edw: Littleton, Esq., Sheriff, a firme man to yᵉ Governmᵗ & a freind to Protestant dissenters.

A spec. verd. intʳ Wright and Dunn* yᵉ pl: brought his ač as schoolmʳ, but showed not his licence, & I was of opin: to ñsuit him, but att Serjᵗ Birch's desire allowed a spec. verd.

A case whethʳ copyhold be wᵗʰin yᵉ Stat: 11 H: 7, C. 20.

---

* Duñ an infamous man, & a clerke in Mʳ. Tempest's office.

Harrington & Smith,* Mes. Rep. 82, 103, 128, 2 Syderf., 41, 42.†

61

An information of a riot ag[t] Hen: Vaughan, Griffin Pain & 19 othrs about y[e] Tolls of Radnor faire, a dispute between Stephens & Vaughan about being bailiff of New Radnor, march[d] 36 men from Keinton to Radnor, 4 miles, on Lord's day in y[e] afternoon.

An ejectm[t] in[tr] Leake & Price upon y[e] will of y[e] Lady Price. An ill verd. p. d.

Att Hereford I entred 38 causes and tryed 35. good Justs., S[r] Edw. Harley, Capt. Scudamore, Ferd: Gorges, Esq. Y[e] B[tt] too favourable to Jacobites, an ill sermon before him att his visitatiō.

*Page 62 blank.*

Att Monmouth.

63

John Floyer, Esq., Sheriff.

We lodged att M[r]. Walt[r]. Fortunes, Major of Monmouth; good lodgeing.

S[r]. Char. Kemys gave me a buck w[ch] he never used to y[e] Judges before.

Good Justs., M[r]. Morgan (a man of a great estate), M[r]. Arnold, Coll. Probert.

My bro: Eyre entred 14 causes & tryed 13.

18 we went to Glocestr, & had a very rainy day & a bad jorney for way over over y[e] forest of Deane & aft[r]wd in y[e] lanes.

64 Gloces[tr].

I entred 43 causes & tryed 39.

Sam. Barker, Esq[re], Sheriff, a freind to y[e] Governm[t].

---

* The case Harrington & Smith is reported Syderfin, 41, 42.

† Les Reports des divers special cases . . . adjudged en le court del Bank de Roy, &c. A.D. 1683. Folio. By Thomas Siderfin. 513. l. 5. British Museum.

M$^r$. Try, undersheriff.

We lodged att M$^r$. Ludlow's or att M. Bell's, a millener, one of y$^e$ Sheriffs of y$^e$ City.

Freinds to their Maj$^{tys}$, S$^r$ Jo: Guise, S$^r$ Ra: Dutton, S$^r$ Duncomb Colchester, S$^r$ Tho. Stephens.

M$^r$. Rowl. Wood, a Just. of P., a good man.

The whole number of causes (besides traverses) entred this circuit was 250, of w$^{ch}$ I entred 128; & of causes tryed was 219, of w$^{ch}$ I tryed 113.

*Page 65 blank.*

66

My 8$^{th}$ circuit was y$^e$ Norfolk circuit. Lent 169$\frac{8}{9}$. 5$^{to}$ W. & M. Ld Ch: Just. Holt & my selfe. Y$^e$ times thus

Norfolk, Wednsday 15 Mar: att Thetford.

Suffolk, Saturday 25 Mar: att Bury S$^t$. Edmonds.

Cambr: Thursday 23 Mar: att Cambridge.

Hunt: Saturday 25 Mar: att Huntington.

Bedford, Monday 27 Mar: att Bedford.

Bucks, Wednesday 29 Mar: att Alesbury.

Aft$^r$ y$^e$ circuits were all setled & y$^e$ terme ended, viz., 25 Feb., there fell a very great Snow w$^{ch}$ occasioned y$^e$ K. to issue out a proclamatiō, 2 Mar. 9$\frac{8}{9}$, to alter all y$^e$ circuits to later dayes, but onely y$^e$ Norfolk & y$^e$ Oxford circuits w$^{ch}$ continued upon their 1$^{st}$ appointm$^t$.

I hired a coach & tooke my chamb$^r$ clerke w$^{th}$ me in it, & by reason of y$^e$ badness of y$^e$ wayes I was forced to take 6 horses & my charges in this circuit for housekeeping & coach-hire cost me out of purse above 52 *li*.

67

We set forward from London Monday 13 Mar: & came y$^t$ night to Hockerill, Bishop-Storford, & y$^e$ next night to Barton Mills, both jornys w<sup>th</sup>out any bate, & att Barton Mills the undersheriff of Norfolk offered to pay y<sup>e</sup> reckoning, but we did not accept it.

68            Thetford, Wednesday, 15 March, 9⅔.

John Burkin, Esq<sup>re</sup>, Sheriff, a sober & frugall young gent.

Wm. Davy, undersheriff.

I sate upon y<sup>e</sup> nisi Prius & entred 23 causes & tryed 21.

*Page* 69 *blank.*

70            Bury S<sup>t</sup>. Edmonds, 18: Mar., 9⅔.

W<sup>m</sup> Hamond, Esq., Sheriff, a sober young gent: his father a merch<sup>t</sup> now living in London, a freind to ptestat. dissenters, he kept a very handsome & generous shirevealty, & gave y<sup>e</sup> Judges gloves, tho there was a woma condemnd, and repreived. — Wright, undersheriff.

My Ld Ch. Just: Entred 47 causes, & tryed 35.

           Cambridge, 23 March, 9⅔.            71

Rob<sup>t</sup>. Swan, Esq., High Sheriff a very old man, and soe his son who had been an attorny officiated in his roome.

James Robinet, undersheriff.

I entred 13 causes & try'd them all, one of them a directed issue lasted in tryall ab<sup>t</sup> 4 houres.

Huntington, 25 Mar., 93. My Ld Ch. J: entred & tryd 5 causes. I tryed 13 prison<sup>rs</sup>.

The same Sheriff & John Johnson, undersheriff.

72            Bedford, 27 Mar. 93.

S<sup>r</sup> Sam. Thompson, Kn<sup>t</sup>, High Sheriff. A young<sup>r</sup> son of his, a Barris<sup>tr</sup> att law, officiated for him.

Ambrose Reddall, undersheriff.

I entred 14 causes & tryed 13.

Ailesbury, 29 Mar., 93.

Fran. Duffeild, Esq., High Sheriff a sowre kind of niggardly man, & (as I am told) a Tory.

Barnwell, undersheriff.

My Ld Ch. J: entred 11 causes & tryed 10: I tryed above 20 indictm$^{ts}$, severall of w$^{ch}$ were for robberys wherein y$^e$ evidence was long, w$^{ch}$ occasioned my stay there a day longer than my Ld Ch: Just. soe that I came not home till Saturday y$^e$ 1$^{st}$ of Apr., '93.

74

In this circuit, my Ld Ch: Justice & I entred 112 causes and tryed 96.

| | | | |
|---|---|---|---|
| I. | Thetford | entred 23 | tryed 21 |
| Ld Ch. J. | Bury | entred 47 | tryed 35 |
| I. | Cambridge | entred 13 | tryed 13 |
| Ld Ch. Just. | Huntingtō | entrd 5 | tryed 5 |
| I. | Bedford | entred 14 | tryed 13 |
| L. Ch. Just: | Ailsbury | entred 11 | tryed 10 |
| | | Total entred 113 | tryed 97 |

Ld Ch. J: entred 63, tryed 50.

I entred 50, tryed 47.

*Page 75 blank.*

76

My ninth circuit was y$^e$ Westerne circuit. Sumer 1693. 5$^{to}$ W. & M:

Ld Ch: Baron Atkins & my selfe. The times thus

Hampshire, Teusday 25 July, att Winchestr.

Town of Southamptō, Friday 28 July, att Southamptō.

Wilts, Saturday 29 July, att New Sarum.

Dorset, Wednsday 2 Aug., att Dorchester.

Cornwall, Tuesday 8 Aug., att Launceston.

City of Exō., Monday 14 Aug., att Exeter.

Devonshire, yᵉ same day att Exeter.

Somersett, Wednesday 23 Aug., att Wells.

City of Bristoll, Monday 28 Aug., att Brist.

I hired a coach & 4 horses, & took my chambʳ clerk in it wᵗʰ me & I was out of purse this circuit above 40 li. in housekeeping, coach, and other exp̄s.

77

Monday, 24 July, 93. I set forward from Lond: into this circuit, and call'd of my Ld Ch: Baron att Kensington, & we came to Farnhā yᵗ night upon an invitation from yᵉ Bᵖᵖ of Winchester, & yᵉ next day we came to Winchester & just as yᵉ High Sheriff met us, one of the horses in my coach fell down dead.

Att Winton my Ld Ch: Baron entred 26 causes & tryed 23; & I tryed 11 indictmˡˢ & 4 travorses.

Edw. Hooper, Esq., Sheriff.

Mʳ Good, undersheriff

28ᵗʰ we went to Southampton, & my Ld Ch. Baron never came into Coʳᵗ there, but I tryed 2 prisonˢ, & allowed one pardon. We had a very handsome entertainmᵗ there att yᵉ Maiors house (Mʳ Smith) where we lodged one night, & on yᵉ 29ᵗʰ we went to Salisbury, & passed by Sʳ Jo: Sᵗ Barbe's new house att Broadlands nere Rumsey in Hampshire.

78                            Salisbury, 29 July, 93.

I entred 31 causes & tryed 26.

Sʳ Tho. Estcourt, Sheriff.

Mʳ. Eyre, und'sheriff.

Wm. Biss, pl., & Edw. Biss, his brother defᵗ. Chan: issue to try if Edw. Biss, yᵉ deft seald a deed 3 May, 70, by wᶜʰ plt. claimed 300 *li*. A verd. p. q̃. ill. onely 2 wīts to it, a markesman who utterly denyd it, & Jo. Alford a feind* Coⁿᵗ hand, he was a Just's. of Peace clerk, his hand was proved by Hen: Mompesson, Esq. uncle to pl. & defᵗ, by their mothʳ who swore yᵗ Tho: Mompess. Esq., his bro. had yᵉ deed above 12 yⁿ in his custody. Rudge sent to inquire in Gloc̆sh: aftʳ Wᵐˢ fortune upon his mar.

For defᵗ, a settlement on his marr̃. with Jane Sims, made Oct: 70: wᵗʰ cerˡˢ by Geo. Biss yᵉ father yᵗ it was not encumbred. Severall deeds showd of Geo. & Edw. wᶜʰ were not like yᵉ hands to this deed. This rased in yᵉ name of Wᵐ. & yᵉ sum̃ & yᵉ words, him, & his. Noe pvision made for any othʳ of the youngʳ childr. of Geo. & Ellenʳ Biss, tho they had severall. Noe jointure to Edw'ˢ wife tho she broᵗ 1,000 *li*. but they expected 3,000.

Tremain & Pawlet, serjᵗ., p d.

Gold serjt. p q̃.

79

The cause of yᵉ Orange Merchˡˢ agᵗ yᵉ Cornish Wreckers for God's goods soe (wickedly) called, high dam̃s 880 *li*. A Trovʳ continued for 2 dayes, & these defˡˢ charged wᵗʰ yᵉ whole tho not proved to be there both dayes.

Seager & Hopkins ac. Sʳ ca. for libell pclaimed in markets & nailed up publikly on yᵉ pillery claiming yᵉ pl. as his wife by a blacksmiths marriage 20*s*. dam̃s onely; ill verd. bec. small dam̃s.

80

2ᵈ Aug: 93. We went from Salisbury & bated at Blanford, 18 miles frō Salisbury att yᵉ charges of yᵉ Sheriff of Dorset, & went yᵗ

* Feigned.

night 12 or 14 miles moré to Dorchester ; we lodged att M$^r$. Tho. Goulds' of y$^e$ house of comõns, close lodgeings, & old furniture.

Jo. Strode Esq., Sheriff.

M$^r$. Shirley, undersheriff. My Ld. Ch. Baron entred 25 causes & tryed 22.

Saturday 5$^{th}$ Aug. We went from Dorchester to Honiton, very rugged Way, we stayed there Lord's Day, & went on Monday to Crediton & on Tuesday to Lanceston. We were not entertained att Bridport as we use to be but had an ill bate at Charmouth.

Launceston, 8 Aug., 93.          81

Hum: Nicolls, Esq., Sheriff. M$^r$. Walker Hobbs or John Littleton, und'sheriff.

I entred 55 causes & tryed 45, & had 2 cognovits.

The Sheriff a firm man to y$^e$ governm$^t$.

82          Att Launceston.

Attorn. Gen. & Cloberry. One Rich. Moile was outlawed in debt in C: B: for 50 *li*. ad̃s of one Williams, & a *spec. cap. utlagatŭ* transmitted into y$^e$ Excheq$^r$ & by an inquisition taken before y$^e$ Sheriff, Moile was found to be possess$^d$ of chattells reall & prsonall. Cloberry came into y$^e$ Excheq$^r$ & pleaded a conveyance made to him by Moile of lands & goods before y$^e$ outlary, & y$^e$ Attorn. Gen: replyed y$^t$ this conveyance was fraudulent, upõ w$^{ch}$ issue was joined, & was tryed before me 10 Aug: & that night y$^e$ Jury gave a private verd. ꝑ d.; but y$^e$ next morning one of y$^e$ Jury disagreed in open Co$^{rt}$ to that verd. soe I sent them back to consid$^r$ of it, but they could not agree of it all that day, w$^{ch}$ was y$^e$ last day of y$^e$ Assizes, & soe att night a Juror was w$^{th}$drawn by consent.

83

We dispatched all o$^r$ business att Launcestõ on Friday, 11 Aug: & came on Saturday from thence to Exeter in a day, & were att Exeter by 6 of y$^e$ clock att night. We bated two houres at Oake-hampton.

84

M$^r$. Ch$^r$. Savory a man qualifyed to be Sheriff of Devoñ p S$^r$ F: D: Tho: Hele, Esq., Sworn J: of P: but acts ag$^t$ y$^e$ Interest of y$^e$ Governm$^t$, a Jacobite, & one who never observes y$^e$ fasts.

Rowl: Whiddon, debauch$^d$ & unfitt.

Y$^e$ Grand Jury, maior pt. of y$^m$ not freinds to y$^o$ Governm$^t$, they publikely complaind of M$^r$. Trout, & some of y$^m$ said y$^t$ severall psons would not act if he were continued in comission. I demanded a list of y$^e$ names of those who would not act, but they gave me none.

M$^r$. Trout a freind to y$^e$ Governm$^t$, sober, of an estate above 400 $li$. p. añ, good understanding, y$^e$ complt ag$^t$ him grounded on a quarrel w$^{th}$ M$^r$. Martin ab$^t$ assessm$^{ts}$. Att 1$^{st}$ backd by M$^r$. Isaac & M$^r$. Stroud of y$^e$ Gr. Jury. All endeav$^{rs}$ could not get 12 to psent him.

Exeter, 14 Aug., 93.

85

M$^r$. Cook, maior  A Tory.

M$^r$. Periam, Sheriff.

I entred 8 causes in y$^e$ City & tryed 7. My Ld Ch: Baron entred 12 causes, & tryed 11. M$^r$. Prestwood, Sher:ff of Devonshire, a drinking Tory. Jo: Etheridge, undersheriff.

We lodged att M$^r$. Southmeads, in y$^e$ Great Street, a mercer, & a zealous Jacobite.

Tuesday, 15 Aug.  S$^r$ Hu : Ackland, M$^r$. Martin, M$^r$. Osborn, & 3 ot$^{hr}$ Justs came to me to complain y$^t$ M$^r$. Abraham Trout of —— w$^{th}$in — miles of Exō was lately made a Just: of P: in Devoñ, who is a pson meane in his extraction, estat$^e$, & qualificat. of understanding for a Just: & disgustfull both to y$^e$ Justs. & to y$^e$ Country. M$^r$. Nic. Morris saith it is a Tory complaint ag$^t$ a Whigg.

86

Thursday, 17 Aug., 93. I went to y$^e$ guild hall of y$^e$ city of Exoñ to try a woman who was charged w$^{th}$ high treason for clipping y$^e$ coine of yᵉ Kingdom, but yᵉ Grand Jury indorsd the bill *Ignoramus*, & soe yᵉ womā was discharged by proclamation. Her name was Eliz. Paddy.

In Devonshire my Ld Ch: Baron entred 90 causes & tryed 65.

Capt. Hodder att Topsham, an old seaman & firme to yᵉ Governmᵗ.

Somersetshire. Aug. 23. Wells.      87

Warwick Bamfeild, Esq., Sheriff.

John Gifford, undersheriff.

Jo. Bale, Goaler.

I entred 69 causes & tryed 51.

Att yᵉ High Sheriff's desire we gave him leave to goe home on Saturday in yᵉ affʳnoon, by reason of his age & infirmitys. My Ld Ch. Baron staid there till Monday 28 Aug., & I stayed till Tuesday 29 Aug., & returnd home to Lond ult. Aug. See before page 21 yᵗ number of causes entred & tryed this whole circuit.

88

My tenth circuit was yᵉ Western circuit. Just. Powell & my selfe. Lent 9¾, 6° W. & M.

The times thus.

Hampshire, Tuesday 6 Mar, att Winchester.

Wiltes, Friday 9 Mar, att New Sarum.

Dorset, Tuesday 13 Mar, att Dorchester.

Cornwall, Munday 10 Mar., att Lanceston.

City of Exoñ, Saturday 24 Mar., att Exeter.

Devon yᵉ same day att yᵉ Castle of Exeter.

Somerset, Monday, 2 Apr., att Taunton.

This circuit we were abroad 5 weekes & three dayes in all, & our table, housekeeping, & travelling (over & above yᵉ givn pvisions & wᵗʰout yᵉ charge of oʳ horses & coaches) cost us 153 *li*. 7*s*: I hired a Coach

& 4 horses, & took my chamb$^r$ clerk in y$^e$ coach w$^{th}$ me, & I hired a horse to carry my portmantle. I was out of purse this circuit above 40 $li$.

*Page* 89 *blank.*

90

Monday, 5$^{th}$ Mar., 9$\frac{3}{4}$. My Bro: Powell & I set forward from Londō upon this circuit, & came y$^t$ night to Hartley Row, but y$^t$ day and y$^e$ next day on w$^{ch}$ we came to Winchestr were very severe, frosty, windy & snowy dayes.

Winchestr, 6 Mar., 9$\frac{1}{4}$. Anth. Sturt, Esq., Sheriff, but we excused his psonall attendance in regard of his son's & his wife's great indisposition in health, and we allowed a kinsman of his, one — Sturt, to act in his place.

Arth$^r$ Good (or Rich: Good, his fath$^r$) und'sheriff, but Rich. Good was also att the time Maior of Winchestr & deputy cler. of y$^e$ Peace.

My bro: Powell Enterd 22 causes, & tryed 18, & I tryed 27 prison$^m$ upon 22 indictm$^{ts}$.

Salisbury, 9 Mar. 9$\frac{3}{4}$. 91

S$^r$ W$^m$. Pynsent, Baron$^t$, Sheriff.

James Townsend, und'sheriff. I entred 42 causes & tryed 41.

An accident befell my bro: Powell in y$^e$ trying of his prison, one$^m$ of y$^e$ Jurymen who were charged w$^{th}$ 5 prison$^m$ (some of them capitall offendors) left y$^e$ Jury & went away, & w$^n$ they were call'd over could not be found: & great inquiry was made aft$^r$ him, but for severall hours he could not be found, & y$^e$ Judge was forced to Swear anoth$^r$ Jury-man & try all y$^e$ prison$^m$ over again, & when y$^e$ missing Jury-man was found, y$^e$ Judge fined him 40 $li$.

*Page* 92 *blank.*

### Dorchester: 13 Mar. 9¾.

*Tho: Cooper, Esq., Sheriff.

Tho: Cooper, under-sheriff.

We had a very plentifull & well orderd diñer given us by yᵉ Sheriff att Blanford in oʳ way to Dorchestr.

Att Dorchester Mʳ. Place† who preachd yᵉ assize sermon, reflected npon yᵉ indulgence by Act of Parl: to Protestant dissenters, and sᵈ yᵉ wisdom of yᵉ nation had givⁿ every man liberty to spit in yᵉ face of yᵉ Church, & had taken away all yᵉ means of correcting strife & envyings in yᵉ Church, & now, *nil nisi vota supersunt*, wᶜʰ seemed to import yᵗ they (calld yᵉ Church) had nothing now left, but onely their old eager desires [*vota*] of persecution. I tooke notice of yᵉ offensiveness of this passage, both to yᵉ Grand Jury in my charge & in my discourse wᵗʰ yᵉ Sheriff, who afterwards told me he was much troubled about it.

94                              Dorset.

Bro: Powell entred 20 causes & tryed 20.

### Cornwall, 19 Mar., 9¾.                    95

Wᵐ Williams, of Probus, Esq., Sheriff.

Walker Hobbs, undersheriff.

Mʳ. Smith, yᵉ minisᵗʳ yᵗ preachd, reflected upō yᵉ indulgence, & inveighd agᵗ yᵉ hypocrisy of them who say yᵗ receiving yᵉ Sacrament kneeling is sinfull, & yet receive it soe to get into an office or imploymᵗ. I heard yᵗ yᵉ Grand Jury desired him to print his sermon.

I entred 29 causes, & tryed 28: & had one *cognovit*.

---

* [p. 92.] This High Sheriff is a button makʳ att Sherburne, & hath got a great estate by yᵗ trade, & still carrys it on, & imploys many hands in it.

† [p. 92.] I have since yᵗ time heard yᵗ this man is a son of Mʳ. Edw. Place, of Well, in Yorkshire.

F

*Page* 96 *blank.*

Exeter, 24 Mar., 9¾. 97

M$^r$. Gandy a brewer Maior. A Tory Bigot.

M$^r$. John Burel, an apothecary, Sheriff, & high Churchman.

Att Exeter Bro: Powell entred 7 causes & tryed 7. I entred & tryed one onely. In Devonsh: he entred 100 causes & tryed——

Devonshire.

Ch$^r$. Savory, Esq., sheriff, a good man & well affected to y$^e$ Governm$^t$.

Tristram Boudage, undersheriff, a Jacobitish Tory.

Y$^e$ D. & Chap: of Exeter refused to let M$^r$. Hodder, y$^e$ Sheriff's chaplin, preach y$^e$ assize Sermon att y$^e$ Cathedrall. They set up anoth$^r$ one, M$^r$. ——* Both y$^e$ judges excus$^d$ y$^e$ Sheriff from comeing to y$^e$ Ch: & my bro: Powell alone went thither.

98

I had great complaints by severall psons ag$^t$ one Tho: Spurway, an attorny, & he was severall times suffion$^d$ to answ$^r$ those complaints, but appeard not, an inform$^r$ in K. J: 2 time; a pson of gen: ill fame. On Saturday 31 Mar: ab$^t$ 5 of y$^e$ clock in y$^e$ af$^r$noon he came to me, but then y$^e$ psons who petitiond ag$^t$ him were gone home as being impatient of staying.

Taunton, 2 Apr: 94. 99

I came from Exeter in y$^e$ morning for fear of losing o$^r$ commission, & bro: Powell stayed to try some causes y$^t$ were upon his hands but he ended them soe as he came to Taunton about 8 of y$^e$ clock att night.

We lodged at one M$^r$. Bird's an attorny & Towne Clerke.

Ro$^{bt}$ Syderfen, Esq., high sheriff, a good man and well affected to the governm$^t$.

Bicknall, undersheriff. I entred 59 causes & tryed 49.

* Blank in MS.

100

We ended y<sup>e</sup> business of y<sup>e</sup> circuit att Taunton on Friday 6 Apr: att noon, & that night one M<sup>r</sup>. Berisford, a young Lawy<sup>r</sup>, told me y<sup>t</sup> some dissent<sup>rs</sup> (I think he named M<sup>r</sup>. Baker & M<sup>r</sup>. Peacock) were much troubled att some expressions of mine in a cause there, between Clare & Bassett, which was an ač. upon y<sup>e</sup> Stat. Ph: & M: for selling Wares in a market. Y<sup>e</sup> def<sup>t</sup> was a poor Townsmā, ruined in Mounmouth's insurreč, & I express<sup>d</sup> my dislike of y<sup>e</sup> psecution, & they told me it was done by some great traders who were dissenters, & I said y<sup>e</sup> psecution was worse in them, than in other men, bec. they had been sufferers und<sup>r</sup> y<sup>e</sup> severe psecution of rigorous penall laws.

101

Western circuit: $9\frac{3}{4}$, Lent :—

| | | | |
|---|---|---|---|
| Hampshire | entred | 22 | tryed 18 |
| Wiltshire | entred | 42 | tryed 41 |
| Dorset | entred | 20 | tryed 20 |
| Cornwall | entred | 29 | tryed 28 |
| Exeter | entred | 8 | tryed.·8 |
| Devonshire | entred | 100 | tryed — |
| Somersetshire | ent: | 59 | tryed 49 |
| | | 280 | |

Just. Powell    entred: 150    `    tryed
Just. Rokeby    entred 130      tryed 119

102

My eleventh circuit was y<sup>e</sup> Western Circuit, Just: Powell & my selfe. Sum̄<sup>r</sup>. 94. 6° W<sup>l</sup>: & M<sup>s</sup>: Y<sup>e</sup> times thus :—

Hampshire, Wednesday 18 July, Winchest<sup>r</sup>.
Wiltshire, Saturday 21 July, att New Sarum.

Dorset, Thursday 26 July, att Sherburn.

Cornwall, Wednesday 1: Aug: att Launceston.

City of Exet^r, Munday 6 Aug. att Guildhall of Exon.

Devonshire, same day att y^e Castle of Exeter.

Somerset, Wednesday 15. Aug: att Wells.

Bristoll. Tuesday 21. Aug: att Guildhall of Bristol.

103

We set out from Lond. Tuesday 17. July, being a rainy morning & we bated att y^e King's Armes att Bagshot & lodged att Farnham Castle upon an invitation from y^e B^pp of Winchester.

Att Winchester we again excused y^e Sheriff of Hampshire's psonall attendance because of his own bodily infirmitys. I entred 20 causes & tryed 19.

Att Salisbury my bro: Powell entred 27 causes & tryed 25.

In Wiltshire M^r. Jifford & M^r. Lewis & M^r. —— 3 Jacobite parsons, have frequent meetings at tan alehouse att —— ab^t 12 miles from Salisbury, & from thence y^e Jacobite intelligence is dispersed.

104           Att Sherburn, 26 July, 94.

I entred 7 causes & tryed 7.

Launceston 1. Aug: 94. My bro: Powell entred 39 causes & tryed 34.

M^r. Fran. Calmady, a good man but too great a charge to be sheriff

105

Att Exe^tr Bro Powell entred 4 causes & tryed 4. I entred 1 & tryed 1.

In Devonshire I entred 93 causes & tryd 63 & bro: Powell tryed 6 for me.

In this circuit Sum̃er: 1694—

|  | causes entred. | causes tryed. |
|---|---|---|
| Winchester | 20 | 19 |
| Wiltshire | 27 | 25 |
| Dorsetshire | 7 | 7 |
| Cornwall | 39 | 34 |
| Exeter | 5 | 5 |
| Devonshire | 93 | 69 |
|  | 191 | 159 |

Wells & Bristoll.

106

My twelfth circuit was y⁸ Norfolk circuit. Justice Nevill & my selfe were y⁸ Judges appointed.

Lent Ass: 9⅘. 7° W: Regis. Y⁸ times thus :—

Bucks, Monday 4. March att Ailsbury.
Bedford, Thursday 7 March, att Bedford.
Huntington, Monday 11. Mar, att Huntington.
Cambridge, Tuesday 12 Mar: att Cambridge.
Norfolk, Friday 15 Mar: att Thetford.
Suffolk, Wednesday 20 Mar: att Stowe-market.

The Parl: sitting, I went y⁸ circuit alone. I hired a coach, a postilion & 4 horses at 22s. a travelling day, & 12s. a lying day, & I put a pair of my own horses to y⁸ wheele, & my own coachman drove. I hired a horse for anoth⁻ serv⁺ who attended on me, & I took my chamb⁻ clerk in y⁸ coach w^th me, & my charges this circuit, ov⁻ & above all rec^ts was 48 li. in y⁸ whole, or very nere it.

The Town of Stow-market pd for y⁸ Judges horsemeat.

Just: Nevile pd noe p⁺ of y⁸ Coach-hire.

1ˢᵗ Mar. 9¾, Capt: Churchill, of Majʳ Gen: Churchill's regimᵗ spoke to me for what men I could pcure him in yᵉ circuit, to goe into yᵉ King's Service in Flanders, & I pmised him them.

Hugh Horton, Esq., Sheriff, a very great grasier, & said to be well affected to yᵉ governmᵗ.

Mʳ. — Barnwell, undersheriff.

I set forward from Lond: Monday, 4 Mar, & dined att Amersham att yᵉ —— att yᵉ Sheriff's charge, and got to Ailsbury by daylight.

I took yᵉ Senior side of yᵉ circuit.

Att Ailsbury Entred by Bro: Nevill's Marshall, Mʳ. Norbury, Six causes, tryed Six causes.

*Page* 108 *blank.*

### Bedford, 7 Mar: 9¾.      109

Sʳ Wᵐ. Massingbeard, high Sheriff.

Ambrose Reddall, undersheriff. The high Sheriff living in Lincolnshire & applying to me att London, I excused his psonall attendance att yᵉ Assizes, & gave him leave to send a freind in his roome, and he sent Jo: Harvey, Esq., a Just of P: in that county.

I entred 4 causes, and tryed 4 causes.

*Page* 110 *blank.*

### Huntingdon, 11: Mar., 9⅘.      111

Arthur Jocelyn, Esq., high Sheriff. Robᵗ. Clark, yᵉ youngʳ, undersheriff.

This high Sheriff was 21 yᵣⁿ old some days afᵗʳ he was named Sheriff, his fathʳ being alive, and a good substantiall farmʳ in Cambrsh., his son married an heiress of about 150 *li.* p añ, & for her estate in Huntingtonshire was made sheriff, and attended me in that county & not in Cambridgshire.

Entred 11 causes, tryed 9.

112             Cambridge, 12 Mar., 9⅘.

Arthur Jocelyn, Sheriff.

Jo. Jeffery, undersheriff.

The coach could not conveniently goe into Trinity colledge, where I lay, soe yᵉ sheriff provided me a chair, wᶜʰ carryed me through yᵉ Coⁿᵗ to yᵉ coach.

I entred 8 causes & tryed 4.

Thetford in Norf: 15 Mar: 9⅘.            113

Francis Wyndham of Cromer, Esq., high Sheriff.

Mʳ. Carter, undersheriff.

The high Sheriff was a gentile young mā of a small estate in present, his mothʳ being alive, a good husband in his shrevalty & it was sᵈ he was made Sheriff upon a pique by yᵉ D. of Norf.

Bro. Nevill's side. Causes entred 11 : tryed 9.

114             Stow-markett, in Suff: 20 Mar: 9⅘.

Daniell Browning, Esq., high Sheriff.

Barth: Paman, undersheriff.

The high Sheriff had been an old Mʳ of a ship, & bought a good estate in this county, & was very rich.

Yᵉ assizes were never held att this place before, & yᵉ small pox being much att Bury, soe as yᵉ Countrey was afraid of comeing there, I was desired att London by Sʳ Jervas Elwys, Sʳ Tho: Barnardiston, & severall othʳ membʳs of yᵉ House of Com̄ons, to keep yᵉ assizes here, wᶜʰ I did in a booth built upon yᵉ ground called yᵉ camping Land, & Lodged att Capt: Bloss his house, & had a chair to carry me to Coⁿᵗ and to Church.

I entred 35 causes & tryed 27.

In yᵉ whole circᵗ entred 75, tryed 59.

N. Entred 28, tryed 24.

R. entred 47, tryed 35.

*Page* 115 *blank.*

116

My thirteenth Circuit was called the Oxford Circuit. Ld. Ch: J: Treby & my self. Justs. of Assize. Sum̄. 95, 7° W: The times thus :—

Berks. Tuesday 9 July, att Abingdon.

Oxon. Thursday 11 July, att Oxford.

Glocester. Saturday 13 July, at Glocester.

City of Glocester yᵉ same day.

Monmouth. Thursday 18 July, att Monmouth.

Hereford. Saturday 20 July, att Hereford.

Salop. Friday 26 July, att Shrewsbury.

Stafford. Thursday 1 Aug: at Stafford.

Worcester. Tuesday 6 Aug: at Worcester.

City of Worces$^{tr}$, yᵉ same day.

I hired a coach & 4 horses, & put a pair of my own to yᵉ wheel, my own coachman drove yᵉ coach, and yᵉ hired mā was postiliō. I took my chamber clerk in yᵉ coach wᵗʰ me, and hired a horse for my servant (Josua Davis) who ridd by yᵉ Coach, & I was out of purse this circuit above all yᵉ incomes, above 65 *li*.

In this circuit yᵉ towns of Abington, Shrewsbury, & Stafford pay for yᵉ Judges horse-meat.

117

| | | | | |
|---|---|---|---|---|
| Abbington. | Ch: J: Ent: | 21 | tryed | 19 |
| Oxford. | Just R. Ent | 23 | tryed | 20 |
| Gloces$^{tr}$. | Ch J: ent | 34 | tryed | 29 |
| Monmouth. | J: R. ent$^r$ | 15 | tryed | 14 |
| Hereford. | Ch Just. entr | 36 | tryed | 31 |
| Shrowsbury. | Just: R. ent. | 45 | tryed | 38 |
| Stafford. | Ch: Just: entr | 25 | tryed | 23 |
| Worcest$^r$. | Just: R: entred | 25 | tyred | 24 |
| | (*sic*) | 225 | | 198 |

Ld Ch: Justice entered    116     tryed 102
Just: R: entr             108     tryed  96

                       224          198

118               Abbington, 9 July, 95.

Ld Ch: Just: Entred 21 causes, tryed 19. Tho. Harwood, Esq., high sheriff, a plain man, having been a seaman, of whom I had noe oth$^r$ character but that he loved brandy.

Moses Burley, undersheriff.

We lodged att old M$^r$. Green's house, he was 75 y$^n$ old, his wife about 42, a grave modest well behaved woman, y$^e$ daugh$^{tr}$ of Majo$^r$ Creed, an old parl: officer who (as M$^n$. Green told me) was kept prison$^r$ in severall prisons for 19 y$^n$ togeth$^r$ af$^{tr}$ y$^e$ restauration of K Ch: 2: w$^{th}$out ever being called to answ$^r$ any crime.

Oxford, 11 July, 95.          119

I entred 23 causes, tried 20.

James Jeñings, Esq., high sheriff. — Heywood, undersheriff.

To Glocester it is reckon$^d$ but 33 miles, *i.ē.* 12 to Burford, 11 to Frogmill (where we bated att y$^e$ sheriffs charge), & 10 to Gloucestr:

Critlet Hill 5 mile frō Glocest$^r$, very risky way, & frō thence to Gloces$^{tr}$ very uneasy coach way.

120              Glocester, 13 July: 95.

Nathaniel Rydler, Esq., high Sheriff, a young gent: well affected to y$^e$ Governm$^t$.

Tho: Webb, undersheriff, a tory. I am told y$^t$ y$^e$ greatest p$^t$ of y$^e$ gentry are well affected to y$^e$ governm$^t$.

My Ld Ch: J: entred 34 causes & tryed 29 causes.

S$^r$ Rich. Cooks, foremā of y$^e$ grand Jury, a warm man & zealous

G

for yᵉ governmᵗ. Sʳ Jo. Guise & othⁿ pleased wᵗʰ my charge, coṁenting on yᵉ act of Rights & libertys.

I fined one Tho. Stubbs 100 markes for seditious words, yᵉ fine was soe little beč, of yᵉ Smalness of his estate, & his great charge of children. I coṁitted him till he paid it.

Monmouth, 18 July.

121

Edw: Perkins, Esǫ., Sheriff.

undersheriff, a consumptive young man.   Not one prisonʳ in yᵉ Gaole, yet my Ld Ch: Just: swore a grand Jury, & gave them a charge.

I entred 15 causes & tryed 14.

A cause between Edwards & Macklen about yᵉ elec̆. of a Maior of Monmouth.   Afʳʳ two houres  spent in it,˙ yᵉ pl: (who I was afterwᵈs told is yᵉ Tory) would be nonsuit, & was soe beč. I would not allow yᵉ inhabiting burgesses to be witnˢ to prove yᵗ yᵉ out burgesses had noe votes in yᵉ electing of a Maior, for I sd they might prove yᵗ by othʳ witnˢ than those who are interested.

122                         Hereford, 20 July.

Arthur Biddulph, Esq., Sheriff, a young gent. sd to be a Tory.

Wm. Badham, undersheriff.

We lodged att Mʳ Williams's, yᵉ cl: of yᵉ Peace.

Here was a famous cause between Birch & yᵉ Bᵖᵖ of Hereford &c. for defaceing yᵉ monumᵗ of Coll. Jo: Birch in Weobley Church, in wᶜʰ yᵉ pł had 12d daṁ.

My Ld Ch: Just: entred 36 causes and tryed 31.

Shrowsbury, 26. July.

123

Ric. Leighton, Esq., Sheriff.

Ric. Mañing, undersheriff

Jones & Loyd a spec. verd. att yᵉ great importunity & upon yᵉ reputat. of Sʳ Wᵐ. Williams agᵗ my opiñ.   Yᵉ q. was upon yᵉ will of

Rob$^t$. Griffith.  A man devises land to A: & his heirs, & if he dye w$^{th}$out heirs of his body, then to B:  Y$^e$ pn$^t$ was wheth$^r$ A. have an estate ta. w$^{ch}$ I affirmed.

I entred 45 causes and tryed 38.

124                 Stafford: 1 Aug: 95.

John Tayler, Esq., Sheriff.

John Blackmore, undersheriff.

Marsh, Goaler.  S$^r$ Charles Wolsley gave me thankes for my charge. My Ld Ch: Just: entred 25 causes and tryed 23.

We lodged att M$^r$ Perry's, my Ld Ch: Just: his Marshall, where we had good lodgings, but those w$^{ch}$ y$^e$ sheriff pvided for us were very mean, as my Marshall told me.

M$^r$. Perry entertained us att his charge, besides our presents we had 3 brace of Bucks & 5 sheep given us.

                Monday, 5 Aug.                 125

We came out of Stafford ab$^t$ 7 in y$^e$ morning & dined at M$^r$. Phillip Foley's att Prestwood, where we had a very noble & generous Entertainm$^t$, & we staied there soe long, y$^t$ it was past 8 att night before we came to Worcester.

126                 Worces$^{tr}$, Tuesday 6 Aug.

Timothy Brigginshaw, Esq., Sheriff.

John Asteley, undersheriff.

I entred 25 causes and tryed 24.

*Page 127 blank.*

128

My fourteenth circuit was y$^e$ Oxford circuit.  My self & Just: Eyre, Justs. of Assize.  Lent 9$\frac{5}{8}$.  8$^o$ Willi 3$^l$.  The times thus:—

                Monday, 2$^o$ Mar., Reading for Berks.

                Oxon: Wednesday, 4$^o$ Mar: att Oxford.

Glouc̃, Saturday, 7° Mar., att Gloces͛.

City of Gloc͛, yᵉ the same day.

Monmouth, Thursday 12° Mar., att Monmᵗʰ.

Hereford, Saturday 14° Mar., att Hereford.

Salop, Thursday 19° Mar., att Shrowsbury.

Stafford, Tuesday 24° Mar: att Stafford.

Worcester, Monday 30°: Mar., att Worcester.

City of Worc̃ yᵉ same day.

I was comãnded to stay att home & Just: Eyre went yᵉ circuit alone.

Horner pᵈ Just. Eyre's Steward 14 li. for my part of yᵉ charges of housekeeping, but I pd noe pᵗ of his coachire, nor Just: Nevill pᵈ me noe pt of my coachire this time twelve month.

*Page* 129 *blank.*

130

My fifteenth circuit was yᵉ Oxford circuit, my selfe & Baron Powys Justs. of Assize. Sum̃er. 96: 8° W: 3.

Yᵉ times thus :

Berks, Tuesday 21 July, att Wallingford.

Oxford, Thursday 23 July, att Oxford.

Glocester, Saturday 25 July, att Glocester.

Monmouth, Thursday 30 July, att Monmouth.

Hereford, Saturday 1° Aug., att Hereford.

Worcester, Wednesday 5° Aug , att Worcestʳ.

Stafford, Saturday, 8° Aug., att Stafford.

Salop Wednesday, 12 Aug., att Showsbury.

In this circuit I hired a coach & four horses & took my chambʳ clerk in yᵉ coach wᵗʰ me. I hired also two horses for John & Josua my two Servᵗˢ, & I was out of purse in yᵉ whole (above all yᵗ came in) above 54 li.

| | | | |
|---|---|---|---|
| Coachire | 24 | 10 | 0 |
| travelling charges into & out of y$^e$ circ$^t$ | 12 | 0 | 0 |
| My share for housekeeping charges | 11 | 0 | 0 |
| Hire of two horses & their meat, &c. | 07 | 8 | 0 |
| | 54 | 18 | 0 |

131

I had made preparations to begin my jorny on Monday y$^e$. 20$^{th}$ of July, but on Friday before, I received a message from y$^e$ Lords Justices y$^t$ I must stay in Town to attend y$^e$ triall of S$^r$ Jo. Fenwick, y$^e$ message was by the Attorny Gen: who told me they intended to arraign S$^r$ John F: on y$^e$ 22$^{th}$, & try him on y$^e$ 25$^{th}$ of July.

On y$^e$ 21$^{th}$, att night, M$^r$. Baker came to me from y$^e$ Lords Justices to acquaint me y$^t$ S$^r$ Jo: Fenwick's arraignm$^t$ was put off till y$^e$ 23$^{th}$ & his triall till y$^e$ 27$^{th}$, & that I must attend it.

On Wednesday y$^e$ 22$^{th}$, ab$^t$ 9 att night, M$^r$ Baker came to me again from y$^e$ Lds Justices & told me y$^t$ S Jo: Fenwick's triall was put off for ten dayes, & y$^t$ I might goe into y$^e$ circuit when I pleased.

On Thursday, 23 July, I begun my journy into y$^e$ circuit, and came well to Wiccomb that night (thankes be to God).

132        Causes in Oxf$^d$ circ$^t$.   Sum$^r$ 96.

| | | Entred. | Tryed. |
|---|---|---|---|
| R: | Berks | 19 | 16 |
| P: | Oxon | 16 | 12 |
| P: | Gloc: | 25 | 19 |
| R: | Monm. | 12 | 9 |
| R: | Hereford | 52 | 43 |
| P: | Worcest$^r$ | 20 | 15 |
| P: | Stafford | 23 | 19 |
| R: | Salop | 60 | 44 |
| | | 226 (sic) | 177 |

| Rokeby | 142 |
| Powis | 084 |
| | 226 |

| Rokeby | 112 |
| Powys | 65 |
| | 177 |

On Friday, 24 July 96, I went frō Wickham to Oxford & that day I dispatchd all yᵉ crown business (but onely giving yᵉ charge wᶜʰ my bro: Powys had done yᵉ night before), but it kept me in Coᵗ till nere 12 of yᵉ clock att night.

Wᵐ. Newell, Jun: Esq., Sheriff, a young raw man, his fathʳ living, a great husbandman (but sd to have 1,000 *li* p añ), yᵉ fathʳ was put on to be Sheriff, but he pcured his son's name to be put into yᵉ Patent (as I was informed), this was his 2ᵈ son, & I was told, he ofñitted his eldest son, because he sd he could not spare him from yᵉ plow.

*Page* 134 *blank.*

Glocester, 25 July, 96.

The way was soe badd from Oxford that it was betwixt 9 & 10 a clock att night before we got to Glocestʳ, tho we came from Oxford abᵗ halfe an houre afᵗʳ 7 in yᵉ morning.

Sʳ Geo: Hanger, Sheriff, a brisk man, & well affected to yᵉ Governmᵗ.

Tho. Stephens, undersheriff.

Langbane, Gaoler.

Here I tryed & condemned Mᵐ Eliz. Biss, a goldsmith's wid. of Oxenhall, nere Newent, for high treason for coining & clipping. She kept yᵉ great mint of all these parts for adulterating yᵉ coin of yᵉ Kingdom. Many tooles & instruments for yᵗ purpose were found in her house. &

many ingotts of silv$^r$ from melted chippings, & much clipt & badd mony, w$^{ch}$ I left in y$^e$ Sheriff's hands. They were weighed in Co$^{rt}$ by M$^r$. Gosley a goldsmith & estimated by him att 338 $li$. in value.

I also att y$^e$ same time condemned M$^m$. Biss's own father, Walt$^r$ Rudge, for clipping.

136

There were severall companys of foot soldiers of y$^e$ Marqu: of Besair's regim$^t$ (who married one of y$^e$ Lord Villers sist$^n$) quarterd in Glocest$^r$ which was kept in y$^e$ nature of a garrison, & every night y$^e$ military offic$^n$ brought us y$^e$ word in y$^e$ evening, w$^{ch}$ was supposed to be a respect to us, as comeing w$^{th}$ y$^e$ King's Comission.

Monmouth, 30 July: 96. 137

Jo: Morgan Esq., Sheriff, a young unexperiencd gen: who came into y$^e$ office to fill up his father's year, who dyed af$^{tr}$ he was made Sheriff; his father (as I was told) was a rich tradesman of Aburgaveny.

I entred 11 causes & tryed 9.

Part of y$^e$ Marq: of Besair's regim$^t$ was quarterd in this Town, & Capt. Pointz, y$^e$ cheife comand$^r$ here, came to me to receive y$^e$ word. I told him I did suppose we were to receive y$^e$ word from them, but he told me in regard we represented y$^e$ King's pson, he was to receive y$^e$ word from us, & accordingly I gave him y$^e$ word: King William.

138 Hereford, 1 Aug., 96.

Very bad & shaking way from Monmouth.

Jo. Long, Esq., Sheriff, an aged gent: who had an estate fell to him lately by y$^e$ death of a relation, w$^{ch}$ brought upon him this office of Sheriff.

Purcell, und$^r$sheriff.

I entred 52 causes & tryed 44.

I being tyred w$^{th}$ my jorny from Monm̃, my bro: Powis alone went to y$^e$ hall to read y$^e$ comĩssions, & before him there was a writ of Assize returnd, w$^{ch}$ was brought by Herbert Croft, gent: ag$^t$ Griffith Reynolds & W$^m$ Dobson, clerk, for y$^e$ office of Reg$^r$ of y$^e$ Deanry of Heref$^d$, & some debate àriseing upon y$^e$ Sheriff's return my bro: Sent to me to come to him, but I sent to him to desire him to adjorn ye Assize in pticular (as well as y$^e$ Co$^{rt}$) to Monday morning w$^{ch}$ he did accordingly.

139

Upon Monday Morning, 3 Aug., 96, I & my bro: Powys being both at y$^e$ Nisi Prius end, I caused y$^e$ writ of Assize to be delivered into my hand, & att y$^e$ desire of S$^r$ W$^m$. Williams, one of y$^e$ pts councell, I caused y$^e$ persons named in y$^e$ panell of recognitors. of y$^e$ assize to be called over onely *de bene esse* to see if they were in Co$^{rt}$, in ca: it should fall out y$^t$ there should be any occasion to use them, for it was thought they could not regularly be called, till y$^e$ ten$^t$ was called to appeare or make defalt, for it was disputed here whether any thing at all could be done, upon y$^e$ return w$^{ch}$ y$^e$ Sheriff made of y$^e$ writt: w$^{ch}$ was y$^e$ very Same y$^t$ is in Newis & Scolastica's ca: Plo: Com: & y$^e$ oldest book of Entre's & Co. Entre's. And it was Strongly insisted upon by Serj$^t$. Birch, Serj$^t$. Geers, S$^r$ Frā: Wiñington & others as *amici Curiæ* (for they would not own themselves to be of councell with y$^e$ ten$^{ts}$) y$^t$ y$^e$ Co$^{rt}$ could not pceed *contra non citatū* for Sum̃s to answ$^r$ is *de Jure naturali.*

140

And S$^r$ W$^m$. Williams, Dobbins, Grove, &*         of Councell for y$^e$ pl: insisted upon Newis & Scolastica's ca Plo. Com.

old Entr.

Co. Pntr.

---

* Blank in MS.

y$^t$ upon such a return y$^e$ ten$^{ts}$ might be called, & if they did not appeare then y$^e$ Assize might be taken by defalt, & upon y$^e$ vieu of those books in Co$^{rt}$ we were both of opinion y$^t$ we might take y$^e$ assize by defalt.

And we pmitted y$^e$ pl: to arraign y$^e$ Ass. w$^{ch}$ was done by Grove in French. And then *Assiza venit recognitura* in Latine was read (onely pt of it to possess y$^e$ Co$^{rt}$ of it).

Then y$^e$ ten$^{ts}$ were called ag$^n$ & appeared & demanded *oier* of y$^e$ writt, & imparled specially till next morning, And then this assize was pticularly adjorned till next morning Tuesday, att 6 of y$^e$ clock.

141

On Tuesday morning (4 July: 96) my bro: Powys came to me into y$^e$ Nisi Prius Co$^{rt}$, & y$^e$ assize being called (w$^{ch}$ was adjornd *de hora in horam*) y$^e$ ten$^{ts}$ appeared, & Griffith Reynolds put in a speč dem$^r$ to y$^e$ Count, & W$^m$. Dobson pleaded *nul tort nul dissaisin*. Upon y$^e$ speč. dem$^r$ we were both of opin: y$^t$ y$^e$ dem$^r$ was good, but we pnounced noe judgm$^t$. upon y$^t$.

That day I tryed y$^e$ issue upon Dobson's plea, & y$^e$ Jury found ag$^t$ him & 50 *li.* dañis. And I gave judgm$^t$ p. q̃. upon y$^e$ verdict *quoad* Dobson, & writ of seizin. But upon Reynolds his dem$^r$ I adjornd it to Serj's Inn in Fleet-Street, y$^e$ 1$^{st}$ day of next Mich: Term.

142

We being straitned in time att Hereford, my bro: Powis went towards Worcest$^r$ Wednesday morning, 5 Aug. I having then 20 causes to try, w$^{ch}$ I dispatchd about 4 a clock y$^t$ afternoon, but came not from Hereford till Thursday morning 6 Aug., 96, but my bro: Powis read o$^r$ cōmission att Worcest$^r$ on Wednesday night & on Thursday morning heard y$^t$ sermon, & charged y$^e$ Grand Jury (on my behalfe), and y$^t$ night I came to Worcest$^r$, & on Friday before diñer I tryed all my prison$^{rs}$, y$^e$ Goale being small.

Worces⁺ʳ, Wednesday, 5 Aug., 96. **143**

Wᵐ Lea, Esq., Sheriff, an aged pson who is a sort of physioian (as I am informed) & by his goeing from market to market wᵗʰ his medicines, hath got a great estate, & for it was put into this⁻ office.

Jo. Jevon, undersheriff. Lately put out of yᵉ Comiss. of Peace & yᵉ Deputy Lieutenancy (D. of Shrowsbury* being Lᵈ Lieuᵗ). Mr. Coventry, son of yᵉ Lᵈ Coventry, Sʳ Jo. Packington, Sʳ Fran : Russell, Mr. Parker, burgess for Evesham & †

**144**

I came out of Worces⁺ʳ toward Stafford Saturday 8 Aug., abᵗ 8 in yᵉ morning, & stayed not by yᵉ way onely att Wolverhamptō, drunk a glass of sack in yᵉ coach (att yᵉ door of an Inn) given us (as is customary) by yᵉ Constables of yᵉ Town, & I read yᵉ Comiss. a little afᵗʳ 8 att night, but my bro: Powis came not in till afᵗʳ 9, & had Flambeaux's to bring him into yᵉ Town.

Stafford, 8 Aug., 96. **145**

John Chetwin, Esq., Sheriff.

Edwᵈ. Bird undersheriff, an elderly man wᵇout cravat or Wigg.

*Page* 146 *blank.*

Shrowsbury, 12 Aug., 96. **147**

Fran : Herbert, Esq., Sheriff.

Jo. Edwards, undersheriff.

Bowyer, Goaler, a very ill man by Sʳ Ed: Leighton's character.

I came hither alone, & ended not all the business till Tuesday 18 att night, & yᵉ next day I went to yᵉ Welsh Harp, & on Thursday I went to Northampton, & on Friday to Dunstable, and on Saturday 22 Aug. 96, to London. I entred 60 causes & tryed 44. See pa: 132 yᵉ numbers of all yᵉ causes entred & tryed this Circuit.

---

* Charles, twelfth Earl and only Duke of Shrowsbury. † Blank in MS.

148

Circuits chosen Thursday, 28 Jan., 96, att yᵉ Excheqʳ chamber :—

      Norfolke Lᵈ Ch: Just: Holt.

      Home,     Ld Ch: Just: Treby, Baron Powys.

      North,     Ld Ch: Baron Ward, Just: Turton.

      West,     Just: Nevile, Just: Rokeby.

      Midland, Baron Lechmere, Just: Powell.

      Oxford,  Just: Eyre, Baron Blencow.

I hired 4 horses & their harness of Tho. Briñ att 20s. a travelling day & 12s. a resting day, & I hired a coach of Norwich Salusbury att 2s. 6d. p working day, i.ĕ., 15s. p week, but it was reduced in yᵉ whole to 4 li.   In this circuit I was out of purse in yᵉ whole (above all yᵗ came in) abᵗ 66 li. 10s.

149

My sixteenth circuit was yᵉ Western circuit.   Just: Nevill & my selfe Just's of Assize.  Lent, 9⅚.   9° W. 3.   Yᵉ times as follows :—

      Southampton, Wednesday 10: Mar., att Winchester.

      Wilt⁸s, Saturday 13. Mar., att Salisbury.

      Dorsett, Thursday: 18 Mar., att Dorchester.

      Somerset, Monday 22 Mar., att Taunton.

      Cornuᵬ, Monday: 29 March, att Launceston.

      City of Exoñ, Saturday 3 Apr. att Guildhall, Exoñ.

      Devon, yᵉ same day, at yᵉ Castle of Exoñ.

150

Before I began yᵉ circuit I was told by some gent: of yᵉ house of Coñis yᵗ Mʳ Ratcliff, sheriff of Devonshire, is a Tory-Williamite, but hath a good undʳsheriff, Mʳ Hull.

I was also told yᵗ Mr. Dyke, Sheriff of Somersetshire had a desire to express some respect to me.

Tuesday, yᵉ 9ᵗʰ of March 9⅚, Justice Nevill & I set forward into yᵉ Western Circuit, & bated yᵗ day att yᵉ King's head att Egham, & came yᵗ night to Hartley Row & y⁰ next day to Winchester. We had two most delicate days to travel in, above what is usual att this time of y⁰ year.

I returnd to London out of this circuit upon Saturday, y⁰ 17ᵗʰ of Apr: 97.

In this circuit Taunton onely pd for y⁰ Judges horsemeat.

In this circuit I was out 40 dayes, includeing y⁰ day I went out, & y⁰ day I returnd.

151

### Winchester, 10 Mar., 9⁴⁄₇.

Alex. Alcorne, Esq., Sheriff. one who (as I am informed) was a while an apothecary att Southampton, but by marrying three rich wives hath now a good estate.

Rich. Good, undersheriff ppetuall.

Skate, Gaoler.

Just: Nevill entred 16 causes, tryed 11 causes. I tryed onely 5 indictmᵗˢ & had one traverse in wᶜʰ noe evidence was given.

There is a difficulty in this County abᵗ the cōmon Goale of it. They say y⁰ King hath noe Gaole att all, but y⁰ house which is used as y⁰ Goale was bought with mony out of y⁰ County stock & was taken in y⁰ name of some gent: of y⁰ County, who by ordʳ of y⁰ sess: for a fine & rent, let it to one Hen. Thorp (a very ill man) who hath ever since claimed to be Gaoler, and lets that house for a Gaole att an excessive rate, & now acts as Keeper of y⁰ Gatehouse att Westmʳ. One*            Preist lately acted as Gaolʳ undʳ Thorpe, & is now a turnkey in one of y⁰ Countˢ of London. In this man's time Tho. Collins, accused of coining got out of prison & is fledd.

152                      Salisbury, 13 Mar., 9⁴⁄₇.

Jo. Beñett, Esq., high Sheriff of Wiltes.

James Edgell, undersheriff.

I entred 34 causes and tryed 29, of wᶜʰ one was by bro: N.

15 Mar. Mʳ. Seymour and Mʳ. Tucker, 2 Justs of P: spoke to bro:

---

* Blank in MS.

Nevill & me to speake to my Ld Ch: Just: Holt ab$^t$ y$^e$ business of Susan Bethell alias Bevin, & Edmund Hungerford, Esq., about y$^e$ leasing affair att Fyfield, inflamed & incouraged by M$^r$. Clark & one Moon, Carpent$^r$ who had made affidavits before my Ld Ch: Just: att Londō.

*Page 153 blank.*

154      ·      Dorchester, 18 Mar., 9⅞.

Tho. Bower, Esq., Sheriff.

Robert Russell, undersheriff. Bro: Nevill entred 18 & tryed 18 causes. We had snowy weather Saturday night & Lord's Day morning: both y$^e$ Judges were forced to sitt in Co$^{rt}$ till past 11 of y$^e$ clock on Saturday night.

I repreived Jane Jones, wife of W$^m$. Jones, found guilty of clipping, there being onely one* witnes who swore y$^e$ fact ag$^t$ her, & had concealed it above a y$^r$, & there was not any clipt money or tooles found, nor any concurring circumstance to corroborate his testimony.

20 July: 97. Jo. Gillingham made oath before Hen: Henning, Esq., that w$^n$ Just. Rokeby came back out of y$^e$ Circuit (Lent 9⅞) through Dorches$^{tr}$, he saw W$^m$. Jones, y$^e$ husb. of Jane Jones & †      who married her sister, pay some mony to y$^e$ clerk of Assizes att M$^r$. Colson's house, w$^{ch}$ he estimated to be 20 *li.* or more.

24 Dec., 97. Col. Trenchard desired y$^t$ Jane Jones (being a very dangerous woman) might not be certifyed for, to be put into y$^e$ circuit pardon.

Feb. 9⅞. I certifyed for some malefactors to be put into y$^e$ circuit pardon, but Jane Jones was not put in.

*Page 155 blank.*

156      Taunton, 22 Mar., 9⅞.

Tho. Dyke, Esq., high Sheriff, a generous obliging man in his carriage to y$^e$ Judges, & well affected to y$^e$ Governm$^t$.

---

* Marke Liñington, of whom I rec$^d$ a very ill charac$^{tr}$ from Coll. Trenchard.
† Blank in MS.

M$^r$. Marshall, undersheriff.

I entred 59 causes & tryed 41. Severall of y$^e$ causes were very long.

Cornwall, 29 Mar., 97.     157

Jo. Barrett, Esq., Sheriff.

Jo. Williams, undersheriff, or else Walter Hobbs.

I entred 45 & tryed 35 causes. Tiñers made a complaint of great want & extremitys, & gave their petition to the grand Jury, who gave it to my bro: Nevill.

158

Causes Entred & tryed in Western Circuit, March, 9⅞.

|  |  | Entered | Tryed |
|---|---|---|---|
| N: | Winchester | 16 | 11 |
| R: | Salisbury | 34 | 29 |
| N: | Dorchester | 18 | 18 |
| R: | Taunton | 59 | 41 |
| R: | Launceston | 45 | 35 |
|  | Civit. Exon. |  |  |
| N: | ... | 9 | 8 |
| R: | ...    ... | 5 | 4 |
| N: | Devonshire | 79 | 60 |
| Just: N: entred |  | 122   tryed | 97 |
| Just: R: entred |  | 143   tryed | 109 |
| Total |  | 265   tryed | 206 |

159

Exeter, 3 Apr: 97. Chr. Bate, Maior, A tory creature of S E S.

Gibbs, Sheriff of y$^e$ City, a grocer of good substance, & faire reputation.

Just: Nevill entred in City 9 & tryed 8. Rokeby entred there 5 causes & tryed 4.

Devonshire.

Jasper Ratcliff, Esq., Sheriff, a Rich scraping merch[t] inclind to Torism. Bant y[e] Gaol[r] ill man.

Wm. Hulls, undersheriff, a fair man. I came from Lanceston in one day, staid 2 hours att Bow, & got to Exeter by 5 of y[e] clock. On Easter. Eve I saw snow on y[e] hills in Devonshire near Oakehampton, 3 Apr. 97.

160

In Devonshire Just. Nevill entred 79 & tryed 60 causes.

Very great complaints, in all parts of y[e] great burthens y[e] Inns & Alehouses lay under by reason of y[e] q[r]tering of Soldiers upon them, & upon y[t] occasion y[e] Inns & Alehouses are forced to provide lodgeing, candle, & small beer for y[e] soldiers, & to pay actually down in mony to y[e]-foot-soldiers 3s. p week each man for their subsistence, w[ch] they are hard put to it, to doe, und[r] y[e] great scarcity of mony, w[ch] is yet stirring in trade, y[e] security w[ch] y[e] Inns have for y[e] mony w[ch] they pay to y[e] soldiers, is an account w[th] their officers, & their notes upon y[e] regim[ts] agents, chargeing them to pay y[e] mony to y[e] Inn-keepers.

*Page* 161 *blank.*

162

Circuits Chosen, Thursday, 10 June, 97, att Cheq[r] chamb[r].

| Norfolke, | Ld Ch: Just: Holt. | |
| Midland, | Ld Ch: Just: Treby. | Baron Powys. |
| West, | Ld Ch: Baron Ward. | Just: Rokeby. |
| North, | Just: Neville. | Just: Turton. |
| Home, | Baron Lechmere. | Just: Powell. |
| Oxford, | Just: Eyre. | Baron Blencow. |

My Seventeenth Circuit was y⁰ West.

Ld Ch: Baron Ward, & myselfe Justs. of Assize, Sum͞r 97: 9°
W: 3. The times thus :—

> Southampton, Wednesday 14 July, att Winchest͡r.
> Wiltshire, Saturday 17: July, att New Sarum.
> Dorsetsh: Thursday 22 July, att Dorchest͡r.
> Cornwall, Wednesday 28 July, att Lanceston.
> City of Exon, Tuesday 3 Aug., att Guildhall, Exon.
> Devonshire, y⁰ same day, att y⁰ Castle of Exon.
> Some͞rset, Wednesday 11: Aug., att Wells.
> City of Bristol, Monday 16 Aug: att Guildhall.

This circuit I hired a coach and 4 horses of Tho. Brind, att 20s.
a travelling day, and 12s. a resting day, & allowed him 2 li. towards
paying for y⁰ coach, & I tooke my chamb͡r clerk in y⁰ coach w͡th me, &
had onley one serv͡t (Josua) on horseback, & I was out of purse (above
all y͡t came in) about 67 li. or more.

I came home w͡th my Ld Ch: Baron by Bristoll & Bath, w͡ch some-
thing increased y⁰ charge: I returned home y⁰ 21: Aug. 97.

164                     Tuesday, 13 July, 97.

Ld Ch: Baron Ward & I begun y⁰ West Circuit & came y͡t evening
to Hartley Row w͡thout bate, & y⁰ next day betwixt one & two of y⁰
clock to Winchest͡r.

                    Winches͡tr, 14 July, 97.                165

Sheriff as y⁰ last Assizes.

Ld Ch: Baron Entred 16 causes & tryed 15. I tried 8 indictm͡ts, &
I tryed a traverse of one Jo: Carnham, alias Carnon (a papist & formerly
a Scotch pedler but now) a rich linnendraper ab͡t Reading, his offence

was uttering counterfeit mony, knowing it to be soe, he was acquitted ag$^t$ a clear evidence. I bound him to y$^e$ good behaviour.

166                  Salisbury, 17 July, 97.

Y$^e$ same Sheriff as last assizes.

I entred 24 causes & tryed 21.

               Dorchest$^r$, 22 July, 97.            167

The same Sheriff y$^t$ was last assizes.

Ld Ch: Baron entred 18 & tryed 17 causes.

168                Lanceston, 28 July, 97.

The same Sheriff y$^t$ was last assizes.

I entred 32 & tryed 28 causes.

Att Poulston Bridge (a long mile from Launceston) we entr into Cornwall.

               Exeter, 3 Aug., 97.              169

Y$^e$ same Sheriff in County, & y$^e$ same Maior & Sheriff in City that was last assizes.

We came from Launceston to Exeter, Monday, 2$^d$ of Aug: but could not forward y$^e$ business by it.

Att Exeter Ld Ch: Baron entred 10 and tryed 10.

In Devonsh he entred 80 & tryed 62. In Exeter I entred 4 & tryed 3.

170

My Ld Ch: Baron & I sate togeth$^r$ in y$^e$ City of Exet$^r$ by vertue of o$^r$ comission of Oier & Termin$^r$ upon y$^e$ triall of one Patrick Cunningham for a misdemean$^r$ for speaking dangerous and treasonable Words, viz., we will take off y$^e$ King's life in y$^e$ wint$^r$ if we canot before, for tho y$^e$ K. hath escaped w$^{th}$ his life now, he shall shortly dye before nine months be to an end.

*Page 171 blank.*

172                    Wells, 11 Aug., 97.

Yᵉ same Sheriff as was last Assizes.

The Judges lodged att Mʳ. Baron's house ovʳ agᵗ Sᵗ. Cuthbert's Church, a great distance from yᵉ Coᵗ.

I entred 39 causes & tryed 34.

In this circuit Ld Ch: Baron Entred 124 causes & tryed 104, besides 13 att Bristoll.

I entred 99 & tryed 87.

Soe yᵗ in yᵉ whole circuit both Judges

|  |  |
|---|---|
| entred causes | 223 |
| & tryed causes | 191 |
| besides Bristoll causes | 13 |


                    Bristoll, 16 Aug., 97.                    173

I receiving an invitation from yᵉ Maior & Sherifs of Bristoll, went thither wᵗʰ my Ld Ch: Baron.  Ld Ch. Baron entred 13 causes & tryed 13.

Mʳ. Jo. Hind, Maior of Bristoll, a sugar baker, a plain man, but firm to yᵉ governmᵗ. Mʳ. Petʳ Sanders, eldʳ Sheriff, merchᵗ.

Mʳ. Whitchurch, youngʳ Sheriff, grocer.

We were lodged att Sʳ Tho. Day's house, he is one of their old parl: men, nere ye Key, his trade is a soap-boiler (as I take it) a considerable man of estate, & firm to yᵉ Governmᵗ, a very spacious house, but inconvenient to me, being 48 steps up stairs to my lodgeing chamber; we were very kindly received by him.

The Mint here hath coined above 300,000 *li.* by yᵉ great care of Major Yates, one of their membʳs in Parl.

174

Mʳ. Edw: Colson, a Bachilor, born att Bristoll, now a merchᵗ living in or about London, hath lately bestowed 12,000 *li.* in building & endowing an hospitall att Bristoll for 12 poor men & 12 poor women.

# TABLE OF ABREVIATIONS.

| | | |
|---|---|---|
| Ab$^t$ ... ... | About. |
| Ac̃ ... ... | Action. |
| Ac. s$^r$ ca ... ... | Action sur le case. |
| Acc$^{ts}$ ... ... | Accounts. |
| Admiss ... ... | Admissus (admitted). |
| Ads. ... ... | Administrator. |
| Af$^{tr}$ | After. |
| Ag$^t$ ... ... | Against. |
| Al̃ ... ... · | Alios. |
| Año. ... ... | Anno. |
| Armig̃. ... | Armiger (Esquire). |
| Arraignm$^t$ ... | Arraignment. ˜ |
| Ass. ... ... | Assize. |
| B.R. ... ... | Banco Regis (King's Bench). |
| B$^{pp}$ ... | Bishop. |
| B$^{tt}$ ... | Baronet. |
| Bro. ... | Brother. |
| Ca. ... | Case, ˜cause. |
| Cap. utlagatū | Capias utlagatum. |
| Cer$^{ts}$ ... | Certificates. |
| Ch. ... | Chief. |
| Chan. ... | Chancery. |
| Ch$^r$ ... | Christopher. |
| Com̃and$^r$ ... | Commander. |
| Com̃iss ... | Commission. |
| Com̃ ... | Comitatu (County). |
| Com̃ons ... | Commons. |
| Compl̃t ... | Complaint. |
| Co$^{rt}$ ... | Court. |
| D. } Def$^t$ } ... | Defendant. |
| D. & Chap. | Dean and Chap er. |
| Dams. ... | Damages. |
| Dem$^r$ ... | Demurrer. |
| Devonsh. ... | Devonshire. |
| Diñer. ... | Dinner. |
| Dow$^r$ ... | Dower. |
| Durhã ... | Durham. |
| Eccles. ... | Ecclesiastical. |
| Ejec. ... | Ejectment. |
| Ent. ... | Entered. |
| Episc. ... | Episcopus (Bishop). |
| Estate ... | Estates. |
| Farnhã .. | Farnham. |
| Ferd. .. | Ferdinand. |
| Foremã ... | Foreman. |
| Foūd ... | Found. |
| Frõ ... | From. |
| G., Gs. ... | Guinea, Guineas. |
| Hill. ... | Hilary. |
| Instr. ... | Instructions. |
| Int$^r$ ... | Inter. |
| Judg$^{mt}$ ... | Judgment. |
| Just. ... | Justice. |
| Justs. ... | Justices. |
| K. Ja. ... | King James. |
| Ld. ... | Lord. |
| ℔ ... ... | Libre (£). |
| Mã ... | Man. |
| Mar. ... | March. |
| Marq̃ ... | Marquis. |
| Marr̃ ... | Marriage. |
| ñ. ẽ. factū | Non est factum. |
| Opin. ... | Opinion. |
| O$^r$ ... | Our. |
| Oth$^r$ ... | Other. |
| p ... | Per |
| p ... | Pro |
| p añ ... | Per annum. |
| pt ... | Part |
| Parl. } Parliam$^t$ } | Parliament. |
| P. and M. | Philip and Mary. |
| pticularly ... | Particularly. |
| ptyes ... | Parties. |
| pson ... | Person |
| psonall ... | Personal. |
| Postiliõ ... | Postilion. |
| pceed ... | Proceed. |
| pclaimed ... | Proclaimed. |
| ptestãt ... | Protestant. |
| pvision ... | Provision. |
| pfits ... | Profits. |
| pp ... | Proper. |
| q̃ ... ... | Querente (Plaintiff). |
| q. ... | Question. |
| R. ... | Retainer. |
| Ret. ... | Retained. |
| Relatiõ ... | Relation. |
| Rot. ... | Rotulus (roll). |
| Sarū ... | Sarum. |
| Sol̃ ... | Soluti (paid). |
| S$^r$ ... | Sir. |
| S$^r$ conc̃ ... | Sur conusance. |
| Spec. ... | Special. |
| Sum̃er ... | Summer. |
| Sum̃s ... | Summons. |
| sd. ... | Said. |
| Sup̃ dict̃ ... | Supradicto. |
| Ten$^{ts}$ ... | Tenants. |
| Trov$^r$ ... | Trover. |
| Ux. ... | Uxor (wife). |
| V. ... | Vide. Versus. |
| V$^s$ ... | Versus. |
| Verd. ... | Verdict. |
| W. and M. | William and Mary. |
| W$^{th}$ ... | With. |
| Westm$^r$ ... | Westminster. |
| W$^{ch}$ ... | Which. |
| W$^n$ ... | When. |
| Womã ... | Woman. |
| Y$^e$ ... | The. ˙ |
| Y$^m$ ... | Them. |
| Y$^t$ ... | That. |
| Y$^{rs}$ ... | Years. |

www.ingramcontent.com/pod-product-compliance
Lightning Source LLC
Chambersburg PA
CBHW031248260626
47169CB00007B/2491